THE ICE MIGRATION

ACKNOWLEDGEMENTS

First and foremost I would like to thank my writing mentor and editor, Jacob Ross. Jacob was the first person to look at these stories, almost fifteen years ago as part of a Spread the Word start to write workshop. Thank you for believing in me.

I am grateful for the subsequent support of various writers during the eighteen years that I have been developing this shape-shifting collection. Special thanks to Joan Anim-Addo and Richard Skinner, my tutors at Goldsmiths University. I am indebted to Richard for his unstinting support, encouragement and unfailing generosity.

Carol Bird, Hannah Davis, Karen Fielding, Lorraine Mullaney and Leila Segal who supported me with the early drafts and have provided a circle of valuable friendship.

I owe a debt of gratitude to Bernardine Evaristo, Maggie Gee, and Alex Wheatle for their guidance and encouragement. They set the bar high and this has kept me striving to improve my craft.

Special thanks to Spread the Word. Their accessible and high-quality workshops have helped me to develop these stories throughout the years.

It has been a pleasure working with Gemma Berenguer of Monostereo – thank you for the wonderful design work for the book cover.

Thank you to Peepal Tree Press for bringing these stories to light and for providing a valuable platform for Caribbean writers.

Finally, I would like to thank my family, Agatha, Ruby, Michelle, Wayne, Tyrone, Joseph, and Mia for the family stories that have helped to shape this collection.

JACQUELINE CROOKS

THE ICE MIGRATION

PEEPAL TREE

First published in Great Britain in 2018
Peepal Tree Press Ltd
17 King's Avenue
Leeds LS6 1QS
UK

ISBN 13: 978-1-84523-358-7

Supported using public funding by
ARTS COUNCIL
ENGLAND

For my sister, Michelle Anita Kaye Wright.

CONTENTS

The Ice Migration Route

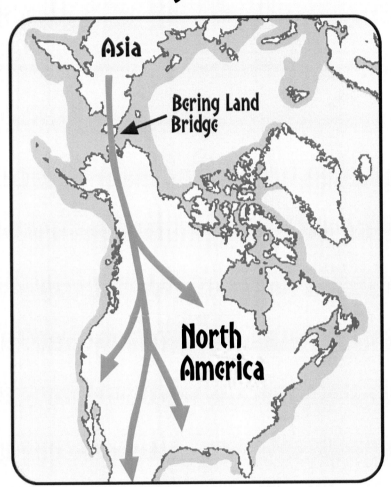

Asia

Bering Land
Bridge

North
America

Bering Land Bridge

Present-day landmass

Landmass that existed
20,000 years ago

Possible migration
routes

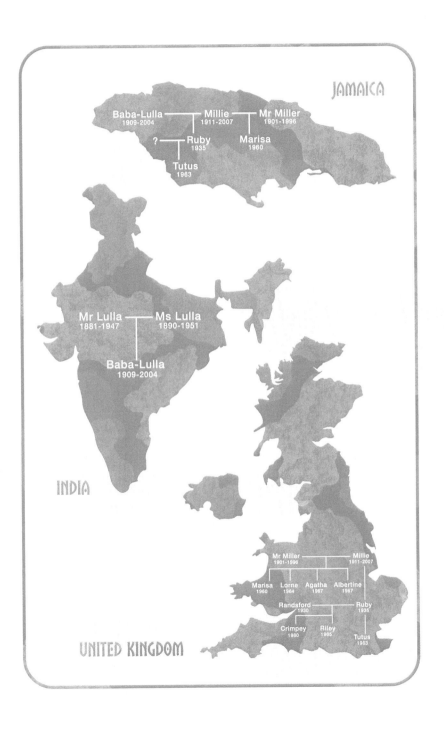

CHIGOE

Roaring River, 1912

Fever-hot afternoon. Sweet-sour air of sweat and cane. Mr Lulla wiped his brow with his facecloth. Watched the black musical notes of cane cutters rising and falling on waves of heat. He hummed a river raga. It distract- ed him for a while, but he was disturbed again by the itching. He looked down at his feet – coral scabs, tur- quoise bruises and white mounds studded like pearls beneath his skin. His feet were decorated like those of Bani, the dancer from Manipuri who carried his music in her jewelled feet.

He crouched, grabbed the big toe of his right foot; squeezed a pearl.

Nothing.

He poked the tip of his machete at the dark pod in the centre of the pearl. Split skin oozed coiled-dead chigoe. 'Where is my God to take me?' he called out.

He must not report sick. Must not run again. Running away that one night had brought shame to his wife. He bit down on his lip, raised his machete high and brought it down with a crack against the sugarcane. He looked across at Ram Baram, Bani's partner, who was grunting and slashing a little way ahead of him.

'Get on with it, old man,' Ram Baram shouted. 'Too much drumming at night. No energy for work. No energy for your little wife.'

Mr Lulla did not reply. You did not reply to a man like Ram Baram.

The bell rang at midday and the overseer, Mr Thomas, rode the black plantation horse around, calling out to them in sing-song:

Come everybody
Mek haste
Mek haste
The massah wan' to
See oonuh face
Come everybody
Mek haste
Fling machete down
Run come along
A deh usual place

Mr Thomas was as black and silky smooth-skinned as the horse, his voice deep and rumbling as Roaring River in the rainy season.

Mr Lulla went with the other men to the accounting barracks. His wife and the other women were already there, motionless in the heat.

Massah Sleifer stood under the shade of the veran-dah smoking a cigar. He exhaled words and smoke. 'You like the sweet water. Sweetness from the sugar. You want more? Some of you came on the SS Ganges. Well, your contracts end just before next year's harvest.'

The Indians waved their hands in the air, shouting. Mr Lulla's river raga came back to him. He hummed it as he listened to the dialects and languages become one hot wavering note.

Massah Sleifer shouted over them. 'The world needs sugar! Give it to them and you'll get land. Sweetness, sweet things. Five more years, that's all.' He puffed more smoke shapes. They floated in the air like white flower-offerings. He turned his back on them and went into the cool darkness of the accounting barracks.

Mr Lulla's wife came to him, her small feet rising and falling quickly, like needles stitching-up the earth. She poked her finger into his arm. 'Land!' she said, and pointed to the mountains.

She was a beautiful woman; her black eyes never showed signs of weariness. Every day he gathered up the dry twigs of his body and burnt himself out on the plantation. But she moved quickly from morning until night – here, there, everywhere – working, talking, scheming. Her black-flitting eyes had wrong-footed them to this place, and he could no longer touch her without losing his sense of rhythm; could not touch his beloved drums for days after.

Bani was shouting, 'If they had told us everything in Calcutta, I would never have come here to this!' Bani was no beauty. Her brown face was long, her nostrils flared. She had the silent, stoic look of a mule. But, oh! when she coiled her plaited hair on her head and danced in the evenings, holding the poses of goddesses – Maya, Shakti, Ganga – perfectly balanced; neck, eyebrows, lips miming a story – every movement a word, words he played on his drums, faster and faster…

Mr Lulla saw Ram Baram go up the steps of the barracks, following Massah Sleifer into the darkness. He did not like the way Ram Baram was moving, his arms tensed a little way from his sides, his hands curved like knife handles.

Bani slid her head from side to side as if she were loosening it from her shoulders. 'I will go home,' she said. 'I will be free. Why would I do it all again? Am I a slave to work like this?'

'What freedom can you have?' Mrs Lulla shouted at Bani. She moved towards Bani with the tiny, sure-footed speed of a chicken. 'You have nothing in Calcutta now. A dishonoured woman, your family would pass you in the street.'

Mr Lulla took hold of his wife's arm. He did not like what she was saying. Bani had been with another man, but she had chosen Ram Baram when the other man left for Kingston, when his contract ended. Ram Baram was a Madrasi. Pockmarked and proud. His heavy brows jutted like a ledge across his sunken eyes. The thin strap of his mouth compressed with curses. A good choice, if protection was all that Bani needed.

The workers crowded around the women.

'A dishonoured woman?' Bani shouted back at Mrs Lulla. 'In this place? Where nobody remembers what castes they belong to? Brahmans, Kshatriyas, Chamars, Dhobis and Doms – everyone working in shit!' She walked away.

Mr Lulla looked on, knowing that his wife would have the last word. Sure enough, she stood where she was – hands on her small hips, elbows jutting like wings – and shouted, 'In this place, a dishonoured woman is like Roaring River when it overflows. No control! It goes where it wants; does what it wants; brings destruction.' Then she turned to him. 'My intuition is never wrong,'

He knew all his wife's sayings: 'It is the hand of God;' 'My intuition tells me such and such…' He wanted to ask how her intuition had brought them to this slavery, but he held his mouth. He wished he could be more like the Madrasis; they were slack and surly. They spoke their minds, fought each other in the hot nights – wrestling oily bodies, bared teeth, stabbing, gouging, scarring. Ram Baram was the worst. Even the overseers were afraid of him.

The men from Calcutta were different. In India, they had worked on flood plains, ploughing, harrowing and smoothing the water-logged rice fields; soaking and beating the indigo leaves until the blue dye released itself into their bodies.

The wind had been stirring up from the north and there was a fiery crack in the air that sent clouds spinning towards them. Rain fell. Quick and hard. Mr Lulla stood in the downpour watching the labourers running, their clothes wrinkled around their bodies like ageing skin.

He ran from his wife, through the darkening rain, remembering the night he tried to escape the plantation.

A crescent moon night. Owls unscrewing the darkness with their eyes. His flat feet slapping the earth as he hurried through the trail-less bush, away from the plantation bell, the overseer's shouts, and the grinding-teeth sleep of his wife. He turned once, saw the retreating pastures of Guinea grass and pangola. He smelt darkness – the juices of the bush seeping into the night. He felt darkness – soft air on his neck, stirring the small hairs on his nape. He imagined Bani naked, lying on the Guinea grass; getting on top of her, entering the wet darkness between her legs. He felt an explosion of power. Ran harder than he had ever run before.

He reached the shelter of the barracks where his son, Baba-Lulla, was asleep with the other children. Rain fell like stones against the zinc roof. The men stuffed rags into rum bottles filled with kerosene and lit them. The women lit the chulah and prepared rice and egg-plant. They passed bowls of food around. Two men, potters from Bihar, said the storm was a sign and they would return to India. Some said they would move to the Indian settlements in Kingston, Bachan Pen and Hindu Town, sell black sugar and bhajji.

Mr Lulla thought that he would have settled for that but his wife snorted, 'Those tin towns! Filled with beggars and crows.'

Others said they had nothing in India now and they would stay on to get land.

Mrs Lulla went over to their sleeping child and pulled the white sheet from his body. 'Look, our son. What do our lives matter? We must get land for him.'

Mr Lulla pushed away his bowl and sat, stroking the globe of his bloated paunch.

Bani stood up. Mr Lulla watched as she pulled her udhni over her head and shoulders. He remembered the journey on the steamship from Calcutta. Bani per-suaded him to play his tabla for the dancing girls from Manipuri. As he played he watched their decorated feet sliding and pounding the deck. And Bani – her rounded body balanced on one supple foot, the other foot crossed against her thigh, arms waving above like a strong, rooted tree.

Mr Lulla wondered what Ram Baram would say. He was bound to the plantation for three more years and would have no woman if Bani left. He hobbled away and lay down in his bed. He smelt the rot of cane trash seeping from his feet. The itching had stopped, he poked out more chiggoes from his feet, noticed dark marks pooling beneath his skin.

During the humid night he shivered and burned, dreamed of naked men, faces tattooed in black, throwing sugarcane spears at him, their sharp feathery spikelets stabbing his feet, pinning him to the ground.

He awoke a few hours before dawn. His right leg was hot and pulsing. He thought of Roaring River, the cool water coasting through the darkness, sloughing the edge off the simmering heat. He got up, walked into the indigo night. He saw red specks of lights in the mountains; heard a horse whinnying a long way off.

He came to the river. Sat on a rock and rested his feet in the cool water. His river raga melody came back to him. He hummed and hummed as daylight began to push through. He stared at the river buried between darkened earth and silver sky.

When he saw her, he was unable to move, unable to stop the raga.

There were river reeds coiled in Bani's plaits and a long line of silver light running along her body. She was floating face down, the water carrying her. A dancing goddess, maintaining perfect balance and stillness.

A sama bhanga.

BLACK COWBOYS

Roaring River, 1921

Harold stood outside the Big House scanning the zemi-shaped mountains that were studded with sink-hole darkness.

It had been raining and the air was wet with the smell of the red earth.

The black cowboys were in the mountains some-where, roasting wild hogs on their hidden, smokeless fires. Not like him, with his bafan legs, the pain in his calves and thighs like teeth clamped around them.

He walked to the river. Baba-Lulla was there as they'd planned, his white cotton trousers rolled up, wading through the shallow part of the river, kicking up black magnetic sand.

Baba-Lulla came to the shore and they sat beneath a canopy of wild banana leaves.

'Cowboys, what do they have to hide?' Harold asked.

'Them more than cowboys,' Baba-Lulla said. 'Living on meat and mannish water. Muma says dat put one dangerous kinda heat in a man's body.'

Harold knew the black cowboys weren't like the riding-roping-stampeding ones he saw in the silent films that his father, Massah Sleifer, used to take him to in the open-air screenings in Kingston. The black cowboys rode the lower mountain slopes, herding cattle for his father. They kept to themselves, camping high-high, on inaccessible ridges of the mountain, beyond the bloodwood trees.

Sancho was the only one they saw close up. He came down to the river with the cattle early in the mornings, and sometimes at night if there was a full moon, like tonight.

The villagers didn't like the cowboys or their horses – 'bad-breed man and dem duppy horse,' they said.

Harold and Baba-Lulla watched and waited until, some time later, Sancho and his white horse clopped across the old Spanish bridge that traversed Roaring River past the yellow limestone church, onto the southern bank. Harold watched as Sancho led the horse further upstream where the water was deeper, rougher. He signalled to Baba-Lulla and they followed from a distance, crouched down in the bush.

The plantation foreman once told Harold that Sancho was descended from the Maroon rebel, Juan Lubola, and African runaways. '*Mix-up man.*' Harold was fascinated by the mixing of blood that had produced this strange-looking man whose skin was the colour of pone – golden-brown and pitted.

'You didn't come last night,' Harold said.

'You did watch him last night as well?' Baba-Lulla asked.

'Twice this week. Too hot to sleep – mosquitoes and every damn thing bothering me.' He wasn't going to tell Baba-Lulla about his night pains; it felt like something he wasn't supposed to talk about.

'Your blood mus' be sweeting them,' Baba-Lulla said.

'Shhh, look.'

They watched as Sancho took off his riding gloves, put his rifle on the ground, stripped himself naked.

Harold stared at the cowboy's thin yellow body, the pattern of tightly packed muscles that covered almost every part of him like a disease.

'What kind of thing goin' on?' Baba-Lulla asked.

'Never done this before,' Harold said.

Sancho led the horse into the river – the same part of the river where Harold and Baba-Lulla used to play with the other plantation children.

Harold was sixteen, skinny and stiff-backed awkward. In the last year or so, something had distinguished him and Baba-Lulla from the other boys, so they were often alone together, and as secretive as the black cowboys. But Harold didn't understand what their secrets were, or where they came from within themselves. His friendship with Baba-Lulla had started at the same time as the pains in his body.

He felt foolish for his superstitious thoughts that the pains were somehow connected to the dreams he had when he caught fevers in the rainy season. Dreams where he saw his body stretched out, stone cold in a country where sky and land were one – an endless mass padded with snow and ice.

Sancho led the horse deeper into the river.

'Him going drown the horse,' Baba-Lulla said.

'No, no. Look. He's making it swim. That's what he's been doing these nights.'

Sancho tugged at the horse's mane, mounted him. Rode him around and around.

The horse stumbled once and Harold put his hand on Baba-Lulla's shoulder as if to steady him, but still he couldn't take his eyes of Sancho. The pain in his legs was heavy and insistent, and there was a feeling of anxiety in his gut that made him think of Trenchton and Gillard – some of the boys they used to play with. Those boys, with their swagger and defined groin muscles, had started bragging, in an almost menacing way, of their 'sessions' with women. Women with strong, square bodies hewn out of the loneliness of their isolated shacks in the middle ridges of the mountains. Women who were broken off from social taboo. Different in every way from his mother, who was small, tawny-eyed and tight-lipped.

Watching Sancho and the horse made Harold feel the same way as listening to Trenchton and Gillard – excited and afraid.

The horse stumbled and fell forward into the river.

Horse and rider were underwater.

Harold held his breath.

Sancho and his white horse surfaced into the blue moon-glow and Sancho mounted the tired animal again and rode him around and around until the horse began to shake.

'Come, mek we go,' Baba-Lulla said. 'The man look like him goin' bruck something tonight and – bwoy – I don't want it to be me.'

Harold didn't move.

Baba-Lulla crouched down again.

Sancho led the horse out of the river. The creature was shivering and snorting, pointing its ears.

Sancho looked around, and Harold and Baba-Lulla lay further down into the bush.

The cowboy patted the horse and it stomped the ground, kicking up the grass and the bush-smell of cerasee.

'Me just gentling you, sah, nice and easy. Gentling you cos you need to be with others,' Sancho said.

'Nobody wanna be lonely and wild, not in this yah valley.'

The horse cried out as it reared.

Sancho pulled the horse's head down and put his mouth to the horse's flattened ears. The horse bared its teeth at Sancho's whispered words, and Sancho worked his hand along the horse's spine, rubbing, stroking.

Harold felt the pain in his legs soothing. He thought of his mother. Why had she never come to him in the nights when he had fevers? His skin burnt red, white-gold hair soaked against his neck.

She was responsible for his pain.

Sancho tethered the horse to a tree and moved behind it, talking in a strange, tight, high-pitched voice. 'Easy now, easy. Me just gentling yuh. Nuthin' more, yuh hear!'

'Come, nuh,' said Baba-Lulla. 'This look like trouble.'

Harold brushed his hand away. 'Go, if you're going.' The pains had started again.

Sancho was still stroking the horse and moaning. The animal shuddered and then became still, its ears turned backwards.

'Me gone,' Baba-Lulla said. 'This is big people business.'

Harold watched him move away, crouching low.

Harold knew that Baba-Lulla would go downstream, back to the black magnetic sands because he, at least, was comfortable in his body. Comfortable on the island.

Harold could not leave. Some secret was about to be revealed. About Sancho, about himself, about the river, about who belonged where.

Sancho was moaning loudly, crying, the raw bawling grating on the pain in Harold's legs. He looked away to the mountains and saw two red-eyed specks high up, parallel but far apart.

But there was still no smoke.

He realised that there would never be any smoke. He took off his clothes and lay, face downward, his limbs spread out on the cool moist soil, his silent tears mingling with the red earth.

BREAKING STONES

Roaring River, 1934

Baba-Lulla saw Millie and her old grandmother sitting under the spreading branches of a guango tree. Their legs opened around a litter of stones. It was Saturday afternoon. The villagers had returned from market hours ago, and were cooking, drinking, sitting on verandas. But Millie and her grandmother worked on.

Bruck-Bruck-Bruccckk.

He heard the grandmother shout out, 'Blisters, bu'n-up batty and bend-up back. For what? Dollar a day! Me body bruck up. It dry! Need likkle river water. Mek it tek me away. Lord! Mek it tek me away.'

Bruck-Bruck-Bruccckk.

He watched as Millie smashed her hammer against the pile of stones.

Bruck-Bruck-Bruccckk.

The grandmother hobbled towards Roaring River with her pail and Baba-Lulla went to Millie.

'Is why yuh watching me so?' she asked. 'You think this yah is slave work, eh?'

From neck to waist she was held together by thin fluted bones.

She threw a small stone at the machete in his hand and said, 'Well, is better than cutting cane.'

Baba-Lulla shrugged.

Millie picked up another stone. It was red and gnarled as a sweet potato. She held it up to him. 'These stones more important than sugah. We making Portland cement. Limestone, shale, mixed with these stones.'

'Cement,' he said.

She drizzled the dust of the broken stones into Baba-Lulla's hand.

He blew it into the air, walked away.

Baba-Lulla cleaned out the boiling house as he did every Saturday. He bathed in the river with some of the other young labourers before going to the bookkeepers' barracks where Harold Sleifer, the young manager of the plantation, was drinking a mug of rum and milk. A half-eaten plate of pickled pig's tongue and potatoes lay by the side of the rusty Remington typewriter on the desk. Harold shunned the cool comforts of the Big House. He spent his evenings in the yard playing dominoes and cards with the labourers, sharing their rotis and rum. His father, old Massah Sleifer, would not have approved. He had died after a strange fever he'd caught in Cockpit Country.

Baba-Lulla leaned against the corner of the desk. 'Hey, Harold, you know, Millie, the stone breaker?'

'You interested in her?' Harold asked. 'Forget it, man.' He closed the accounting book. 'Her people go to the Trinity Church. Triple trouble.'

Baba-Lulla looked at Harold's thin red lips. He remembered Harold's shattered grey eyes the day they had spied on the wild black cowboy. He was scared that what they had seen would, in time, bring out something terrible in them. But there was always the rum.

They drank several mugs of the overproof rum before joining a game of dominoes out in the yard.

Baba-Lulla haunted the river bank that night.

Overcome with rum, he sees a body rippling and flowing in the movement of Roaring River. He throws a stone into the river, breaking up the image.

Millie, the dust duppy, comes much later. She strips and washes the dust from her body, but it's no use, she is still as much a duppy as all the women he sees in the river. Women who have danced, cut cane, made coffee, broken stones.

Millie holds out her raw, blistered hand to him and smiles.

He sees the whiteness of her teeth in the darkness.

They lay on the river bank, invigorated by the sound of underground water.

Baba-Lulla's lungs fill with the smell of blood and pimento grass. He has broken Millie. She is his now.

Millie worked all afternoon and just before dusk she went in search of her grandmother.

She was not in their shack, slumped on her mattress of river reeds. She went to the shop and Post Office in the village, searched the sugar plantation and the river bank.

The sun fell on the horizon, splintering into reds and purples.

The grandmother slipped out of the shadow of dust. She waded into the clear, cool river, singing:

"Rock of ages,

Cleft for me

Let me hide myself in thee…"

She felt clean and young again. She smelt limestone, porous with ancient spirits.

She reached out to the women floating beneath and they pulled her towards them.

THE ICE MIGRATION

Roaring River, 1963

Baba-Lulla had not seen Millie since harvesting time four months ago. They had not been together as man and woman for many years. That Sunday morning, he was looking down into Roaring River village, an area of rolling pastures based on limestone hills, bounded on the north by the sea. The bell from the old Spanish church was ringing through the valley. He saw Ruby, their child, running up to his mountain house with all the wasteful energy of youth: her arms churning the air; shaking her head of twisted Afro-Indian curls that bore the deep-rooted scent of her muma, Millie. They sat together on the veranda.

'Poopa, I going to England with Muma and Poppa-Miller. I make up me mind!'

Baba-Lulla looked at her. Ruby was a facety young woman who, six months ago, gave birth to his first grandchild – a daughter named Tutus. His mouth moved, but no words came. There was nothing he could say. He looked to the sky where a plane was leaving a trail of white. Going to be plenty snow where they going, he thought.

His own Muma used to tell everyone that he, Baba-Lulla, was a seer – able to see into the past and future through his visions. But he could not see where this journey would lead for Ruby, for Millie, for himself.

He knew the details of his parents' journey. 'Two weeks of rough seas,' his mother had said. 'A storm, blue like Indian sapphires.' Twelve hundred moaning Indians, sick with fevers, vomiting and kaka. He saw his mother in her bunk, coiled like a seahorse, holding herself tight.

Six months later, when all the preparations had been made for Ruby's journey, Baba-Lulla walked down the mountain to meet her. It was early and the morning mist was slipping down the mountain towards the valley. He was travelling with Ruby and the baby to Kingston airport. Millie was travelling with her husband, Mr Miller.

Baba-Lulla knew little of Mr Miller, except that he was a Trelawney man. Millie had a child with him, Marisa, who must be around three now. She was to be left with someone in the village.

His mind was on Millie as he came out into the shining valley of flame of the forest and golden shower trees. He walked past the silvery slabs and gantries of the sugar factory, struggling against the brightness.

He came to the bus shelter, a run-down hut where slaves and Indian labourers once lived. Ruby was standing outside the bus, shouting at the driver.

'No, man, my grip coming inside with me.' She was stomping the ground with her white stilettos, kicking up red dirt. 'Me not putting it on the roof – What! when I know people luggage always flying off down dat mountain?'

'Come, nuh, Ruby,' Baba-Lulla said, and he took the baby from her arms and guided her onto the bus.

The bus pulled off an hour later, filled with passengers fanning themselves. They drove through Moneague, Ewarton, banana plantations. Baby Tutus slept on his lap, stunned by the heat, the swaying and jolting of the bus in and out of potholes. He stared at the scenery that flicked by, like a motion-picture spooling towards the end of its reel.

At the airport, Baba-Lulla and Ruby stood back from the crowd.

'Well, me child, this is it, eh?'

'Poopa, I going to write; don't you worry.'

'Here, take this, so you don't forget me,' he said. He took the gold bangles from his wrist and gave them to her. 'My muma wore these when she left her people in India.'

He remembered his mother shaking her bangled hands at him. 'Listen, son, I shook off my caste, see; I left it with the Port Officer when that ship left Calcutta. Only the cane left for me to fight.'

Baba-Lulla wondered what fights Ruby and Millie were going to. He watched as men straightened their trilbies; women, wearing long white gloves, fumbled in their handbags for tissues.

Millie was dressed like a river, blue cotton flowing around her hips. She was walking slightly away from Mr Miller, who held on to his hat as if it were about to fly off. His woman – he still thought of Millie as his woman – had the usual look of stout independence. Her lips, pursed with their secret sensuality, made him want to call out to her. But he knew the chemistry of love, like the chemistry of spices, was no easy thing to understand. He watched as Ruby walked towards them, with Tutus in her arms.

The plane took off and the coarse black hairs on Baba-Lulla's arms shot up. Rain goin' fall tonight, he thought. He wondered if any of them would come back.

He watched as the plane moved towards the sun – an insect embedded in amber.

He went to the New Lucas Inn, a small bar just outside the airport. He drank nine shots of white rum. He drank until he saw dark, hooded figures struggling through snow. He drank until warmth swelled up and pulled the flesh around his bones. He heard his mother's voice again: 'Only the cane left to fight...'

Then came the vision of the steamship emerging from white mist all those years ago, after six months at sea. His parents carrying sari, rug, dhoti and drums. A winch pulling up crates as steam blasts from every orifice of the ship. His parents being loaded onto a rusting open-top truck with a group of others and driven along narrow roads shaded by ferns and bamboo.

He sees himself as a child watching his father cutting the fifteen-foot rails of cane that fence them in. He'd joined his father on the cane fields when he was fourteen.

It was a few days after his coming of age celebration that Baba-Lulla asked his parents about the family in Hariharpur, India. 'Dada, why you never write to them?'

His dada, who was shaving with a mirror cotched between the roots of a silk cotton tree, said they could not; how could they when they had broken the lines of their forefathers by leaving India?

Mrs Lulla sucked her teeth and said, 'Son, get paper and pencil. Today we send message.'

When Baba-Lulla came back with the paper, it was Mr Lulla who dictated it:

Respected family, we write from the other side of the sea. We have a son. Pray for us at the holy river. Please write. Respectful greetings.

Baba-Lulla addressed the letter to Village Hariharpur, District Bahraich, U.P. India.

The next morning he took the letter to the Post Office.

His father started going into the vale once a month. He made excuses for going into the store-cum-Post Office. He needed this and that lotion, he said. He always came back with a brown paper bag full of tamarind balls, lung tonic for his wife and writing paper for Baba-Lulla.

There were never any letters from Hariharpur.

Two months after Ruby's departure, Baba-Lulla received a letter dated 19 December 1963, from 33 Alexander Avenue, Southall, England.

'Dear Poopa, I hope very much that you are well. Southall full of Indians – just like you. Plenty-plenty coloureds and poor white people too – what a something! Snow falling every day. Tutus bawling every night because of the cold. Not a blessed donkey in sight, but a rag-and-bone man come every Wednesday in him cart with a mash-down horse. We did go up-town to take our pictures. I will send them with my next letter.'

He wondered how they all looked now in that strange land – England – with snow falling in their eyes?

He tried to imagine Southall, relating it to things he knew: cotton fields, cane ash, mountain streams; rumouring rivers with drifting logs and river plants idling the day away. But instead, he saw images of the remnants of his parents' past – whenever he looked at their blue woollen Himalayan rug that was now beginning to fray.

Ruby wrote once a month for five years. After she had the second child, the letters dwindled to once a year at Christmas.

Baba-Lulla continued writing to her up until his vision started to blur. The rum was working its way through his body. The trails of white beneath his eyelids were growing longer and longer.

His sight was almost gone.

It was Saturday afternoon and Baba-Lulla was in the Roselle rum shack, sitting on a stool at the circular bar. There were tables around the bar. Men were slamming dominoes against a table with the same purposeful, heavy movement that Millie used to break stones.

Baba-Lulla was deep in a mist of smoke and rum fumes, and on the radio a presenter with sing-songy patois clipped with high English was saying something about a special feature. Baba-Lulla heard 'lost cultures', 'time and space', 'things that are left behind'.

He thought of Ruby, Millie and Tutus. His chest tightened and he leaned forward, rested his breast against the bar. With each word of the presenter: 'lost', 'migration', 'left', 'behind' – Baba-Lulla felt the wounds, deep inside him being scoured.

The presenter was talking about the Tainos, his speech building up into a commotion of big words. The coarse-grained voices of the domino players rumbled on. Rickety tables shook. The presenter's voice got faster and faster.

Baba-Lulla felt the room vibrate. The men at the table looked like primitives with flints in their hands, knocking them against rock. The last thing he heard: 'Tainos came from Asia, travelled through Siberia, along the Pacific Coast during the Ice Age, across secret ice passages… a lost trail has been found… beneath the sea…'

He caught his breath and closed his eyes. The trail of white behind them thickened, and he saw their shapes emerging from the white fog. The same dark-hooded figures he has always seen. Dancing patterns of snow and wind moving against them.

He wondered whether Millie, Ruby and Tutus would ever turn back on that old trail – the ice migration. He had stayed behind. There are always those that stay. The only place for people like him is up inna mountain – up inna the air.

'All this coming and going,' he shouted out. 'Man, this island confused by time.'

The men are used to the shouts and cries of drunken old men. They pay him no mind. Baba-Lulla wants, more than anything, to see Ruby, Millie and Tutus again. But he knows he never will. The cane took his sight two years ago.

'Diabetes,' the doctor said. 'Too much rum.'

The only thing he sees is the trail of white.

BACKRA

Roaring River, 1965

Harold Sleifer was reading in his armchair near the bedroom window. On the mahogany card table with the other photos and books, was a tintype photo of his mother as a young woman. An image created with iron and varnish. Pink tint on ghost-white lips. He remembers her like that – a negative standing against the dark corners of the Big House, watching.

It was early afternoon and the tropical sunlight came in through the jalousies at sharp burning white angles. Harold shifted the chair away from the window.

He rented two rooms at Poinciana Pension House in Balaclava town near the old railway station. The rooms were furnished with Spanish elm and blue mahoe and smelled of the mimosa that the owner, Mrs Solomons, grew in the yard. His small inheritance meant that he did not have to work again, so long as he lived this simple life. The town suited him. Here, he wasn't the son of Massah Sleifer, the backra of the sugar plantation. He could spend his days reading about the Maroons and their ambushes.

But sugar was in his blood and today he was reading about the history of sugar: the white trail from New Guinea in 8,000 BC to the New World. Moving from luxury to necessity. A medicine, preservative and condiment. Sweetening and spoiling relationships.

His childhood memories of the plantation were filled with labourers' shadows flickering with silver and gold. The Big House filled with the smell of baking and simmering coffee. Big Maybelle, the live-in help, certainly wasn't a shadow. She cooked, baked and brewed coffee all day long. His father drank it constantly: strong in the morning; medium-strength in the afternoon; milky coffee au lait with sugar to settle him at night.

Harold did not have the taste for it at all.

He would be fifty-five next month. It was the thing he feared most: the adumbratio that shaded his every move.

Some hours later, there was a knock at the door of the sitting room and the helper, Miss Nicey, called out that there was someone to see him. He was afraid it was the shake dancer from several nights ago. He could still feel the sweat-shimmer that had highlighted her black androgynous body in the darkness.

He went through to the sitting room and was surprised to see a young, light-skinned woman.

She wore a bright green dress with a wide-tiered hem fanning her calves. Something familiar about the freckled face. She smelt like one of those up-town women, who dusted their bodies in snowstorms of khus khus talc.

'Can I help you, young lady?'

She said her name was Eudes, and she was Big Maybelle's niece. 'Big Maybelle sick,' she said. 'She send me to come look fe yuh.'

There could only be one reason why she had come to him, he thought: money for a doctor, hospital or a funeral. 'Very sorry to hear it,' he said.

He motioned for her to sit on the planters chair. He wondered how much money he should give. He had not seen Big Maybelle for some forty years. She had travelled with his family from Seaford Town to Roaring River, but had returned to her family in Mandeville some years later, when he was still a boy.

Harold remembered Big Maybelle fussing over him: giving him crude wooden toys, baking him patties, boiling herbs and pulping roots when he was sick with fever. During the rainy season he caught fevers, had spectral visions of Tainos painted with red serpents and exposed, burning hearts. He was left clawing the blankets and screaming into the darkness of his room.

It was always Big Maybelle who came to him.

He took fifty American dollars from his wallet and gave it to Eudes. 'Get her anything she needs,' he said. 'Write if you need more. And please send her my good wishes.'

Eudes took the money, put it in the orange frou-frou bag that she clutched on her knees. 'Big Maybelle seh she want see yuh.'

'See me?

'She deh in her yard, inna Mandeville.'

'I have business here,' he said. 'I can't just go running to Mandeville.'

'Big Maybelle seh I must tell yuh she have important business wid you.'

Harold said it was impossible, and the young woman sighed, 'Oh Lord.'

He pulled out his wallet again.

Eudes stood up and said, 'Well alright den, I going tell yuh the business. If you nuh want come, is fe yuh business.'

Harold stepped away from her towards the white light. He didn't like the way Eudes was smiling at him, as if it was he that was sick.

'Yuh is Big Maybelle pickney,' she said. Her voice was sing-songy, a lullaby. He was fascinated by its cadence even as he leaned back on his heels, and laughed. He could not stop laughing. He did not stop her from leaving.

Over the following weeks he went about his business. Played dominoes and drank rum at Hortense's Bar. Once, he almost made a joke of it to his dominoes partners.

The things women will do to get hold of a man's money!

He thought of driving to Roaring River to see Baba-Lulla. But when he thought of what he would say after so many years, his tongue took on the shape of his heart and his heart spoke of what he could not begin to understand.

So he slept with the shake dancer from the Carib Bar. In the middle of the night the woman dressed and left to go back to her children.

It was then, in the dark strange night, the woman gone, that he felt the world spinning away. He tried to ground himself, thinking about Dusterdick, Eisinger, Volker and Zwinkman – the German families his mother had said were lost to them when they moved from Seaford Town to Roaring River.

He lay in the bed rolling from side to side.

In the morning he got in his Lada and drove east.

At lunchtime he came to the fishing village of Alligator Pond and stopped outside a restaurant called Chin Yee's. A small man was leaning against the doorway, looking towards the shore. The man's face was a mixture of Chinese eyes and African nose with nostrils wide as portholes, his head a netting of long, straggling hair. A half-caste. Half. Incomplete. Was that what he was? He almost turned back.

Chin Yee approached the car. 'Evening, Sah, Little bit o' fish tea is what I cookin', if you want a likkle.' He wiped his hands on a corner of his speckled apron. 'I cooking fe the fishermen down deh so.'

Harold looked to the shore where two fishermen were sitting in the cave of an upturned boat. They sat like stunned survivors of a shipwreck. He looked at them and wondered whether it took a disaster to wipe out a part of history that was best forgotten. He ate the fish soup that Chin Yee brought out to him on the wooden trestle. The fish was so fresh he could taste the life in it. And the escallion that flavoured it had the taste of the night from which it had secretly grown.

His imagination was choking him and he could not breathe. He paid for the half-eaten food and left. He drove on past Gut River and Canoe Valley.

Eudes opened the door to him. She was wearing a flouncy pink apron over a grey dress, and her thick hair was tied back with a piece of creamy lace, which pulled her brown eyes up into an exaggerated look of surprise.

'Eh-eh,' she said, 'so yuh come.'

She took him into a small, dark room, furnished with a bony chair and a cedar dresser bearing a bowl filled with pulped root. There was a pallet bed on the far side next to the larger bed in which lay Big Maybelle.

Big Maybelle was no longer big. Her grey-blond hair was pulled back, holding her face together with a certain resignation. Her café-au-lait skin was shrivelled like the skin that forms on hot milk. Her eyes, nose and mouth were European. The only signs of her black ancestry were the grains of tight hairs around her temples.

Harold remembered a woman's face leaning over his childhood bed; hands pulling his face against a breast, where the smells of nutmeg, cinnamon and coffee suffocated him with their spicy warmth.

'I've never forgotten you,' Big Maybelle said. 'Me son,' she said, again and again. Her voice still big, still resonant.

He could see the mound of her wasted body rising and falling beneath the faded tropical patterns of the bedspread. Her sigh sought him out from the darkened room.

He stepped towards her, afraid but curious. The chair was only an arm's reach away from the bed. He pushed it further back and sat down.

Big Maybelle told him of her 'relations' with Massah Sleifer. Mrs Sleifer had claimed the child. Big Maybelle said she had stayed on for a long-long time, but as the years went on and Mrs Sleifer failed to have a child she became bitter and cruel to her.

'The obeah man warned me, "Maybelle, if you stay in that house Sleifer's wife will throw grave dust on your life." So me had to leave,' she said. 'But me could nevah tek you from that good-good life.'

He was irritated by her superstition. But he said he was sorry for her pain.

'You is me son and me never forget you,' she said. 'Me can go in peace now.'

But he knew that she had not released him.

Big Maybelle called out to Eudes. 'Bring him soursop juice and gizadas.' She turned to him. 'You always liked them when you was a bwoy.'

How could the truth come so late? He remembered his white mother – short, silent and saintly. And Big Maybelle, striding about in her bright cotton frocks. And his father! A man obsessed with order and the sugar plantation. '*Homogenized* landscape,' his father used to say, when talking about the plantation. His father had been right. Up to a point. The fields were geometric – squares, triangles and quadrilaterals. But on the northern and eastern margins, one or two were broken up by the occasional limestone hill.

Harold knew that all he had to do was put out his hand to her. Pull her into his life. He lifted his hand slightly off his thigh. There was tension in his wrist. He twisted it and it cracked. He put his hand back on his thigh. He was afraid that her dying breath might strike a fever within him. Her lips were red and when she spoke her breath smelt like the pulped leaves that were placed on her body.

He wanted to cry – for himself.

What should he do? Come again? Give her more money? Oh, why had he come!

'Oh me bwoy, jus' look at you, eh. You turn out so good, eh?'

He could see what Big Maybelle wanted. She wanted fifty years of holding him. She wanted him in her history – an impossible chronology.

He had grown up on the plantation. Left to his own devices, he'd played with Baba-Lulla and the other labourers' children. Those same children had grown up to cut cane when he took over as manager after his father, Massah Sleifer, died. He had built a sick bay for the workers, hired a nurse from the village, built separate living spaces for men and women, and private huts for couples. It had been a sad affair when the estate closed down. The owner, who lived in England, became over-confident when sugar prices rose. He went wild, buying all manner of new machinery for the estate. A year later sugar prices slumped to twelve pounds a ton. The new machinery was sold and replaced with rusting machines.

'But what a way you favour your father,' Big Maybelle said. 'Oh, your father!' And she laughed with a memory.

He was annoyed at her unspoken indiscretion. Ashamed. He could see nothing of himself in her. He was the image of his father – squat, blond hair, grey eyes. He resented the resemblance now. Did not want to look like anyone. Did not want to look at anyone. But he did.

Big Maybelle fell asleep, her mouth open, white at the corners, the smell of her illness seeping from her body. He left, grateful that there would be no goodbyes. No remedy for her or him.

On the drive back to his rooms, he made a detour and drove to Roaring River. It was a full moon and there was a collage of scaly silver on the river. He looked at his reflection in the water. He thought of all the times when, as a child, he had wanted more than anything to be part of the black and Indian boys who played together. He had his position: above them. But he envied them their small intimacies.

He lit a cigarette and stared in the river until his image darkened.

THE LAMP

Roaring River, 1966

Ms Rosalita, the Post Mistress, stood on the veranda holding her lamp and watched Marisa as she walked barefoot, in her thin cotton dress, towards the river. Cockerels were crowing in the rust-coloured light of dawn.

She needed water for cooking and cleaning, but the child was maaga and weak and she always came back with a half-empty pail, having spilt most of it on the walk back.

'G'lang, pickney,' she shouted.

The child still had the muck of sleep in her eyes. Blind as well as dumb. A pickney who never opened her mouth. The child's head must be full of duppies. What a thing! All the child good for was petting dutty donkeys, trailing in their wake like a mosquito.

Mosquito One
Mosquito Two.
Mosquito jump inna hot callaloo!

She wished she would jump into something and dis-
appear from her life. Her stomach acid burned when
she looked at her. The pickney always reminded her of
Carlos, her beautiful boy. Things hadn't turned out the
way she expected – all these feelings – when she agreed
to look after Millie's child.

Carlos was tall, brown-skinned and talawa as any
bush man. He had gone to Florida fifteen years ago
to work in the orange groves, but the hard work and
fierce sun had drained the life-force out of him. The
Sunny Juice people buried him and posted his possessions to her, including the brass lamp that she gave him
before he left.

She burned the oil lamp night into day, every day.

The barking of dogs criss-crossed the deep purple
valley. A few village mongrels were sprawled out like
rocks under the blood-red sorrel bush. Descendents of
the attack dogs the Spanish had brought to the island
five hundred years ago to nyam up the Tainos, but
these mongrels didn't resemble their boasty mastiff
and greyhound ancestors. They were maaga and red,
like the red-skinned child – who was redder than usual
because the day before she had her packing gungo peas
in the buttery, while she stamped postal orders next
door. The corrugated iron roof of the buttery was a hot
griddle and the pickney was the sizzling meat in the
bitch heat of the day. Now, she was burning up with
fever. Burning up the way Carlos had burned in the
orange groves.

A breeze stirred the flame of the lamp and the sharp
orange light quivered with a small dark shape at its
centre.

Ms Rosalita's hand trembled. The acid burned in her

heart this time. 'Dip yuhself in the river, child. It will cool yuh down!' she called out to Marisa.

She had built her house on the sale of gungo peas, healing oils and stolen postal orders. She steamed open letters from England, Canada and America. The stories of snow, factories and fall-outs fed the hot afternoons and the damp, misty mornings. She was a respectable widow in her horn-rimmed glasses and her flowery crimpelene dresses. She went to church on Sundays, sang as loud as anyone else; prayed as loud as anyone else – for her beloved Carlos.

The dogs on the other side of the valley were howling now. She looked up at the sun and back to the child. She was the same height that Carlos had been when he first started to go to town with his father. It had pained her to watch him moving away from her into the shining valley.

'Mek haste, child. I need a full pail before I can start the day,' she shouted.

One of the sleeping mongrels pricked its ears, stretched its back and shook its body.

Ms Rosalita watched as the dog trotted over to the child.

Ms Rosalita sensed the danger, just like she'd known something bad would happen to Carlos.

'Don't go, child,' she had begged him on the morning of his departure.

'Mooma, stop yuh foolishness. I goin' to cut orange, not cane. American dollars. A chance fe the good life. I goin' come back with sumting pretty fe yuh. Nuh true, Mooma?'

She gave him the lamp, which she packed into a box, and a hamper of bullah cake and bay rum. She put her hand out towards him and stroked his brown face. It wasn't her way to cry.

She watched now as Marisa, balancing the pail on her head with one hand, put out the other towards the side of the dog's body and stroked it.

The dog turned its head and sank its teeth into the child's arm.

The child fell to the earth and began to scream, the dog jumping around her, snarling and barking.

One of the village boys ran out from his shack and threw a stone at the dog's head and it ran into the bush.

'G'lang,' the boy shouted. 'Ugly daawg.'

The Post Mistress ran to Marisa and picked her up. Blood was running down her arm onto her dress.

Marisa's fever worsened in the night. The Post Mistress sent one of the village boys for moon-cold river water and she mixed it with bay rum and mopped Marisa's face, and the back of her burning neck. She put her in her own large bed – not in the buttery where she was usually put to sleep.

She spooned river water into the child's mouth through the night. She did not quench her own thirst. She held herself upright. The muscles on her forearms twitched; her palms burned. She dipped her hand into the bowl of river water on the bedside table, turned back to the bed and reached out her hand to the face that was now pure red and gold.

'Muma, Muma.'

'Yes, Carlos, I am here now,' Ms Rosalita said. 'Don't fret now, don't fret.'

She saw her son's beautiful brown face on the pillow, the eyes wide and sulphurous.

She turned up the wick, picked up the lamp and

shone it on his drenched face. His neck was straining, and the veins in his throat stood up. Sweat poured out of him. She put her face close to his and smelt his breath. He opened the black hole of his mouth, shaped it around something enormous, before it collapsed.

'I know, son, I know,' Ms Rosalita said.

At dawn, when the dogs began barking, the lamp went out.

Ms Rosalita began to cry.

WALK GOOD

Southall, 1967

Muma-Miller had endured many things in her forty-two years, but last night, when she came home from the factory and could not move her fingers to turn the key in the lock, well, that was the limit! She kicked at the door until Poppa-Miller's shadow finally darkened the frosted window pane.

'Open the door, man, mek haste and open the door, nuh!' Why did he move like he had molasses stuck between his batty?

'Me coming,' he growled. But his shadow did not move any faster. He opened the door and she sucked her teeth and rushed past him, upstairs to the sleeping children: Lorne and Tutus.

She mopped Bay Rum on their foreheads as they slept. Then she went downstairs and brewed two gallons of ginger tea for their breakfast the next day. It was part of the ritual back home in Roaring River when, during the rainy season, fevers fermented in the river. She knew what to expect from rivers. Snow, here in Southall, was altogether different.

It snowed all through the night and into the morning. She kept the children from school.

Later in the morning she shook herself into Poppa-Miller's duffle coat, pulled his grey balaclava over her head and topped it off with her church hat – the white one with the net. She was layered with vests and four pairs of his long socks. She had stepped inside his skin, and did not like the smell at-all, at-all. No matter how she washed his clothes she could always smell goat-hide, saw-dust and overproof rum.

She went outside the front door and stood for a moment on the step. Maybe she should not go. After all, who would blame her if she stayed at home beside the paraffin heater? Seven months pregnant and she was double the size she had been with Lorne. What kind of baby was she going to have? 'Please God,' she muttered. 'Don't let it have a bullet-head like Poppa-Miller.'

She walked to the gate. Lady Adelaide Road was smothered, shapeless. She heard snow falling off a tree somewhere, like the sound of faint, arrhythmic drum-beats coming from a long way off.

She remembered Baba-Lulla, how he used to play his drums for her. The way he whispered her name, *Millie*, when she told him it was over. She felt the bile of resentment and regret rising in her stomach. Remembering how he had called out, 'Walk good,' even though it was he who had been walking away, down the vale, past the church, the village and the dull bronze of over-grown cane fields, heading up to his mountain.

No, she had to go out. She needed meat (she imag-ined a side of pork cooking by Roaring River – on pimento wood, spitting fat). She walked into the white haze and her breath was crushed. Things would have been different with Baba-Lulla. Oh God, she had loved that man. But maaga as he was, he was trouble when he was drunk.

Baba-Lulla was a coolie: dark skin, soot-black hair, a nose thin as macca stick, with two pinches for nostrils. Sugar had claimed him.

She used to watch him playing his drums with his eyes rolling in their sockets, like a blind man happy to let go of colour and shape.

The rum from the cane had cut the flesh from his body like acid.

She broke stones; Baba-Lulla cut cane.

He got drunk; she prayed.

The more she thought about Baba-Lulla, the more disorientated she became in the snow. She skidded, spun, and caught herself. There was only the awful silence, like the day when he had asked her not to leave.

There had been a series of baptisms several weeks before. The Pastor had worked his way through the hesitant, the curious and the resistant – a crusty-faced man, with a bullet head and lips as dry as salted cod. This man was pushed forward by his mother who had come all the way from Secret Cove.

She watched as the stranger was held up on either side by Pastor and the Deacon. They pulled him backwards into the water. He was pulled out, eyes bulging, cheeks puffed like a bullfrog.

This bush-man is re-born, her family said. Mr Miller is a good, steady man, who listens to his Muma.

When no answer came from her, Baba-Lulla had told her to 'Walk Good.'

She'd felt as cold as stone in that hot day, watching

him walk away, his thin body like charcoal, smearing the limestone hills.

She made it to The Broadway and leaned for a moment against a lamp post, outside the butcher's.

'Aie, Baba-Lulla,' she said, 'Aie.'

She went inside. 'Two pound a' cow foot, please, Sah.'

The butcher was as heavy as a sea cow with the same sad eyes. He noted the weight of the meat before rolling it in newspaper.

Muma-Miller counted out the pennies and handed them over with a sigh. These were the three things she fretted about: food, fuel, and snow. Meat was so expensive. She had to buy the scrags – cows' feet, pigs' trotters and chicken wings. And then the big old house needed so much paraffin. What if the paraffin heaters burned the house down, like the house on Alexandra Avenue, killing the twenty-three Indians who had been cooped up inside three rooms? She was glad she had not left Tutus on Alexander Road with Ruby and her new man. Oh, but there were so many things to worry about.

In Roaring River she used to step-it with Baba-Lulla to Secret Cove market – twenty miles and more away. They strolled barefoot along dry dirt tracks, and in the rainy season they slithered together through red mud.

Walking in snow was a more slippery affair. Cho! she was too old to be learning new tricks.

She stepped out of the butcher's. The roads were empty, the streets dotted with dark, bowed figures who did not seem to be moving. She went past the bowling alley and the Palace Cinema. She should get back home, fry the meat, rub-up cornmeal dumplings, boil green bananas for the children and Poppa-Miller.

She stepped into the road in a bluster of icy wind, at the centre of a body of cold dry air. A force. She tried to stand still. She felt swept up into the air. Was this happening to her? She put her hands out; felt nausea rising from her stomach up into her throat.

Then she was on the ground. Everything was wet: the duffle coat, her hat and her elasticated baggies. Her waters had broken. Three months early and the baby was on its way! Lord help its soul.

At the hospital, the baby finally came out like a cork from a bottle.

The doctors whispered and shook their heads. The baby was taken away.

Muma-Miller was about to close her eyes to say a prayer when she felt pain cut through her back. 'Whaaaiii!' she shouted; and then she pushed. Something as black and hairy as a ball of wool rolled out.

Another baby.

This baby made a feeble mewing as it, too, was taken away.

Then, what seemed like hours later, something slithered out of her. She rolled onto her side. It was mottled with blood and slime.

The two surviving babies were not expected to make it through the night.

'They weigh less than a bag of sugar,' said the midwife.

'Sugar, eh?' said Muma-Miller, and she fell into a deep sleep.

Poppa-Miller came to the hospital after his shift. He wore a suit and the green trilby with the feather perched on the side like a question mark.

She gave the cotton-wool child to him.

'Here, tek this one; she favours you.'

He took the child and nodded his head. 'Agatha,' he grunted in his thick voice, which sounded as if phlegm and patois had got mixed up.

Muma-Miller held on tightly to the first child – the bigger, prettier one. 'Albertine,' she said, determined not to be outdone. 'This child is Albertine.'

Agatha and Albertine survived.

The third baby was never mentioned again.

CORNMEAL DUMPLINGS

Southall, 1968

Back then, I was often looking for her.

It wasn't easy in that big old house. That day I found my grandmother, Muma-Miller, in the kitchen, steaming it up with back-a-yard food.

Blackened pots hung from the wall, the open sideboard weighed down with loaves of hard-dough bread and logs of earth-encrusted yams. She was kneading cornmeal on the blue formica table. Her brown hands moved as if the purple pumping veins, twisted through her hands like electric wires, were the only things making movement possible.

'Come, Tutus,' she beckoned, 'I rubbing-up your favourite: cornmeal dumplings.'

We sat together at the table and I helped roll the dough into willy shapes. I remember that we worked in silence, rolling shapes between our palms, our hands slipping in and out of prayer. She plopped the flabby dumplings into a Dutch pot of simmering stewed peas. We stood by the stove, with the golden cornmeal on our hands, as if we had spent the afternoon building sandcastles on some faraway shore.

'Listen, Tutus,' she said. 'Every girl must know the secret of a good-good dumpling.'

She whispered the secret and then the next thing I knew, she was shaking her floury hand in my face, saying, 'But I warning you child – don't tell people our business!'

In a house where the adults never talked directly to each other, it seemed, back then, as if everyone was minding their own business. Muma-Miller talked to the sky when she was vex. She would look up, feet hip-width apart, her weight slightly more on the right hip – the good one – waiting, as if she could be transported to another planet where a white God, sitting on a throne, would ask for just one more sacrifice before he could really make things right.

Uncle Trevor came at the weekends. He was the only white uncle we had. A novelty in those days of small-town, sixties segregation. He came in his nylon cravat and slimy drainpipe suit and was always given the best chair in the back room. This room had a fake marble coffee-table, a tilting radiogram and a glass cabinet filled with gold-rimmed china.

Uncle Trevor snoozed in the bat-winged armchair, his hairy fingers crouched on the Paisley print. He had a beef-tomato shaped face. Uncle Trevor was the boyfriend of Marjorie, the Barbadian tenant who lived downstairs. Marjorie was a nurse who moved around the house with a nurse's efficient, confidential air.

On the days that Marjorie came home late, Uncle Trevor waited for her in the back room with Poppa-Miller. The two of them snoozed side by side in front of the horse racing on the hired DER TV, their snores jumping over furlongs of nose hairs, falling back at the water-jumps of phlegmy throats, then out again, blustering from stale open mouths.

Uncle Trevor brought us Irish potatoes and carrots because he had his own greengrocery.

'Eh-eh, businessman, my dear,' Muma-Miller said to Aunt Ermeldine. 'A white businessman. Heh, Marjorie doing well.'

Aunt Ermeldine said, 'Businessman? Businessman my back foot! More like a busy-man, busying himself in other people business.' She folded her arms against her stony breasts and nodded her head to one side. It was not what she said. It was the look, the nod, the turning away of the face.

After they were married, Marjorie and Uncle Trevor lived in Marjorie's room. 'Until business is sorted out,' Uncle Trevor told Poppa-Miller one Saturday, over the drone of horse racing. 'I'm in-between 'ouses. Selling up, buying up, yeew know. I'll give a little extra for the rent.' But Poppa-Miller had nodded off.

Of course, we children were interested in nothing but other people's business. The opportunity came early one morning. Muma-Miller was praying (out loud) in the back room. Poppa-Miller was on the early shift at the factory. We could smell burning hair, so we knew Aunt Ermeldine was in her room, straightening her hair with the iron.

We crept downstairs to Marjorie's room. All the rooms had old-fashioned brass locks with large keyholes, where once there must have been elaborate keys. When they bought the house, Poppa-Miller had hammered in crude bolts on the insides of the doors – presumably so people could lock their business inside. We took turns, peeping through Marjorie's keyhole.

I saw Marjorie bending down over the bed. Uncle Trevor was pushing a carrot into her bottom. 'No, Trevor, no,' Marjorie kept saying, as if she were asking one of her patients to get back into bed.

Uncle Trevor kept on poking and probing. His bristly eyebrows touching each other across a ridge of concentration.

We took turns to watch and covered our laughing mouths with our hands. We knew this was business we had to keep to ourselves.

I kept the secret for several weeks.

One Friday night, Muma-Miller hosted her usual prayer meeting in the back room. Poppa-Miller had his domino nights there on Saturday and they all drank white rum and slammed dominoes on the fake marble table, beneath the picture of Jesus. That night I heard the murmured prayers and the ecstatic shouts of 'Hallelujah!' from the prayer group. I was in bed with the other children. I heard the front door bang several times late in the night, as the prayer group left. Then it was quiet.

I couldn't sleep.

The loose window creaked inside its frame. A cardigan sleeve hanging from the sewing machine looked like a limp arm waiting to come alive. And Albertine, the strange twin, would soon start talking in her sleep.

The bedroom door rattled. We children didn't have a bolt on our door. The adults didn't think we had any business to mind. A draught came through as the door opened. Uncle Trevor came in and closed the door. He crept to the bed. Lorne was snoring at the bottom; the twins, Albertine and Agatha, were woven together like jippa-jappa, in the corner against the wall. I was at the edge of the bed. Uncle Trevor whispered, 'Albertine, you awake?' A pause and then, 'Agatha, it's Uncle Trevor. Are you sleeping?'

Then he came to me.

I should have pretended to be asleep. But at that age I didn't know how to use my intuition.

'Yes, Uncle Trevor,' I answered when he called my name.

'I've got something for you,' he said. He stepped closer, stooped and put his face close to mine.

I don't remember if he used the word 'secret' or if I guessed it from the way he spoke, through pursed lips, pleading and hissing. He raised himself slightly and pressed the secret into my hands.

'I love you,' he whispered. 'Your Uncle Trevor Loveess yeew.'

I held on to Uncle Trevor's secret as he raised himself, his head spinning from side to side like a giant. I held on to his secret until I had the feeling that I could make him fall with my hands. I held onto the secret until my arm was as heavy as a rock. I was a child carrying the secrets of Lady Adelaide Road, of Southall, of Roaring River village where we had come from.

Of the whole world.

I did not know how to let go.

Uncle Trevor was concealed in the shadows and I could only see one side of his head, lit by a stab of light coming from the window.

The secret was slipping through my fingers. I couldn't hold it any longer.

'Hold it, and get rubbing,' Uncle Trevor hissed.

Rubbing? Who said anything about rubbing. Rubbing was for cornmeal dumplings. It was the thing Muma-

Miller did with her brown hands – rubbing until she had a dough that would break off into dumplings, dumplings that would feed everyone in the house. I knew how to hold a secret. Rubbing it was a different thing. It had me on the verge of tears.

And then the voice came from the darkness: '… because it opens when the shadow says…' It was Albertine, talking in her sleep again.

Uncle Trevor crept from the room. He took the secret with him.

In the morning I went in search of Muma-Miller again. I found her in the kitchen. The frying pan was on the stove filled with bubbling oil. She was making fried dumplings and callaloo. Her hands were covered in white flour and she was breaking off and rolling the dough into white, beef-tomato shapes. I stood the way I had seen her stand, legs planted as wide as I could get them. I pursed my lips just like Aunt Ermeldine, crossed my arms against my flat chest and nodded my head to one side.

'Muma-Miller,' I said.

She looked up.

'Uncle Trevor…' I said.

'What is it, Tutus?'

'You… you… are not to tell Uncle Trevor your business,' I said. Then I nodded my head again. I hoped she would understand.

But she laughed – a long deep-belly laugh – and said, 'Come, Tutus, come help me rub-up more dumplings.'

TALKING BAD

Southall, 1971

Lorne was ramping with Mikey in the peach-coloured afternoon, down at Bush Tea Canal. He knew Poppa-Miller would bruck him up for being late. But cho!

Bush Tea Canal was his 'talking bad' name for the Grand Union Canal. Bush Tea Canal because it was as green as the cerasee tea that Muma-Miller brewed to wash the badness from his belly.

In the distance, beyond the woods, he could see the Callard & Bowser sweet factory. That was next to the Mother's Pride bread factory, and that was next to the Wall's sausage factory. Factories belching fire. One big dutty fry-up. He shook the jam jar and the maaga grey fish floated in the dirty water with its bass-bulging eyes.

'It's dead,' he said to Mikey.

'Blimey, that was quick. They never live long, do they?' Mikey said. He turned out his empty net into the canal. 'She could 'ave stayed, you know,' he said to Lorne.

Tutus had followed them as usual that morning,

trailing behind as they walked on the path through the park. Leaves were snowing in the autumn sunshine. Children upside down on climbing frames. Blood draining into their faces.

They turned along the towpath to the bridge and Lorne told Tutus to go.

'Stay in the park,' he told her. 'Muma-Miller says you're too small for the canal; you might drown.'

'But I'm with you.'

'I always have to look after you. Can't you leave me alone for once?' Lorne said.

Tutus' lip trembled and she rubbed her fists into her eyes. The sky above them was bright blue, the sun sharp as a lemon. She was wearing a cardigan over one of her frilly dresses, white with silly ribbons. Lorne didn't like the way she was looking at him. It felt like the heat from the sun, warming and exhausting him all at the same time. He watched Tutus walk away. She wouldn't cry and she wouldn't turn back, he knew that. But she would find him again in the afternoon. She was hard-ears stubborn, just like Muma-Miller said.

He and Mikey had carried on, past the woods, over the wooden footbridge down to the canal side, to their usual spot.

Mikey arced his fishing net over the murky water and let it fall.

'What about Ingrid? She's not here,' Lorne said.

'Me mum's been crying. Again. Ingrid's staying indoors with her,' Mikey said. He looked up to the sky. 'Tutus loves you,' he told Lorne.

The word 'love' sounded strange to Lorne. He didn't know if there was a word for love in the dictionary of talking bad, patois. Muma-Miller and Poppa-Miller never talked about love; all they seemed to talk about was rivers of blood. They were worried they were going to be sent back home, to Roaring River. Lorne looked at Mikey and felt a throb in his throat. Rivers of blood. New decimal system. Everything was changing and he didn't like it.

He poured some of the canal water from the jam jar into his hand. 'What would happen if we drank it?'

'It's poison! Look at the bleedin' fish,' Mikey said. 'Poor things ain't goin' nowhere.'

Lorne looked closely at Mikey. He knew that he and Mikey were friends because he, Lorne, was black and Mikey was grey. Their nails were black with the same dirt. Mikey and Ingrid wore grey balaclavas and trench coats. Their muma cooked tripe in a blackened pot over the fire in the grate and their house was full of creaking dark furniture. Muma-Miller called Mikey and Ingrid the 'grey pickney'.

Lorne wanted to tell Mikey about the language of his singing and praying house – the talking bad. The Caribbean wailing, flexing and shay-shay moves. But he was ashamed. He skimmed the surface of the canal with his net and let it drop close to where a rose petal floated by with a cluster of red leaves.

What if Tutus went to the other side of the park and picked up the canal there? She couldn't swim. Nor could he – but he would style-it-out – he wouldn't be scared like her.

'What's that?' Mikey shouted. 'Look!'

Lorne looked in the direction that Mikey was pointing, far down the canal, just before the bridge. Something white floating there.

He heard Muma-Miller's voice in his head, 'Bwoy,

you mek her drown. Whooy! Al-mi-gh-ty-Jesus. How me fe live now.'

'I'll get it,' Mikey shouted.

'Don't!' Lorne called out, but Mikey was running. A matchstick-boy sparking off the autumn light.

Mikey used his fishing rod to pull the white thing nearer to the bank. He shouted to Lorne and waved his arms in the air.

Lorne ran towards him, into the sunlight. A liquid pain in his belly, the frowsy smell of Bush Tea Canal filling his mouth.

It was nothing but a huge hunk of polystyrene. Discarded packaging. Someone had been buying something shiny and new with decimal money.

'Cor! Just look at it,' Mikey shouted. 'It's big as a bloody raft. We can sail on it.'

'You know I can't swim,' said Lorne. 'Nor can you.'

'Who needs to swim? It's a raft. Anyway, me dad's taken me swimming.'

'No he hasn't.'

'Ask Ingrid, she'll tell ya!'

What a lie. Lorne hated it. Mikey was always skinning-up like his belly was full and his house warm. Mr Baines hadn't taken him swimming. Neither of them had fathers like that. Mr Baines did one of two things when he showed up. He went to the Three Horseshoes pub to gwap-down beer. Then he went home to bruck-up Mrs Baines. Lorne had seen her liquorice black eyes and swollen gob-stopper lips.

'We're never gonna catch any pike here,' Lorne said.

Two boys streaked by on bright bikes, like silver fish from an ocean. They shouted something as they sped past. Mikey leaned over the edge of the bank and used his fingers to pull the raft to the bank, his face almost touching the water. 'Here we go, here we go, here we go. Come on, don't be a sissy,' he said.

'Not me,' Lorne said. The dark water was without end. Just like the prayer at the end of Sunday school, when Pastor said, 'World without end.' Or was it, 'Word without end.' It didn't matter, whatever the words were, they made him feel like he was in a sicky-sicky place where he couldn't breathe, couldn't run, couldn't speak.

Lorne stood back and Mikey climbed down onto the raft and knelt in the centre. Knees bent, small arse sticking out, his fishing rod held horizontal.

Lorne looked down on his friend. They'd always done everything on a level: concentrated, down on the floor, knees in the dust rolling marbles; standing tall, aiming and knocking conkers. Side by side with their cheap fishing nets, pulling dead fish out of Bush Tea Canal.

Mikey straightened himself. 'Me dad says the canal goes west down to the River Colne. That's where his mates are; that's where he stays – most o' the time.' He poked the rod against the side of the canal and pushed off.

'We come from Roaring River,' Lorne said. 'Maybe you can get there. Betcha it's better than the River Colne.'

'Nah. I'm gonna find me dad.'

'What if he's not there?'

Mikey didn't answer.

Lorne watched as Mikey sailed away on the polystyrene raft. He watched him until he sailed through the canal tunnel into darkness. Lorne sprinted along the towpath. He felt the fluids in his stomach sloshing from side to side; his breath surging up from his ribcage, through his nose and into his head, scattering all his bad words. When he was parallel with the tunnel's end he leaned forward, hands on his knees, panting. Bile filled his mouth. When he'd caught his breath he shouted, 'Mikeeeeee!'

He waited. And waited. The white polystyrene floated out from under the bridge.

Lorne listened for Mikey. He heard the sounds of children's voices coming from the playground on the other side of the canal, brittle, sweet, rising up, cracking the lemon light.

Clouds drifted away from the sun. The light sharpened and beamed onto the canal before disappearing into the silence beneath the water.

Lorne was stomping and flexing, acting out the words that wouldn't come. When finally they came, he didn't know what he was shouting. He heard his voice high up in the light. Then the words melted on his tongue.

There was a splash. Circles within circles within scum. Small bubbles like frogs eyes. Froth. Stillness.

A man's face surfaced from the depths of the canal. His fringe like a blindfold across his eyes. 'I can't reach him,' he said. 'Get help. I'm going down again. God help me.'

It took them four hours to find Mikey and cut him free from the canal weeds that bound his feet.

'Yuh not going to see no dead body,' Muma-Miller said that night. 'Yuh is a child. Yuh no have no business with death! Mek haste and gwaan to yuh bed. Yuh not goin near that dutty canal again. Yuh hear wheh me say, pickney.'

Lorne crept out through the back door early in the morning. He heard Muma-Miller and Poppa-Miller in the kitchen. They were talking bad. They were talking about death and duppies.

Lorne walked quickly along the cobbled street of terraced houses and coal bunkers. The morning air was bombo cold but there was a woman on her knees, rubbing the stone doorstep with a red rag.

Mikey was laid out in the parlour of his house. He was wearing his grey flannels. A burst-blister look about his face. Something thick and sweet seeped out into the room, full of people. Neighbours, Mrs Baines' relatives, the local bobby, drinking tea, shaking their heads and tutting. Not a tear. No one was speaking bad.

Lorne looked at Mikey and wondered who he'd really been in the darkness of his bedroom. Mikey's father, Mr Baines, walking his slow coffin-bearer walk, coming into the room with bloodshot eyes, further darkened the house that was always dark with soot and sadness. .

Lorne kept thinking of Mikey trapped in the depths of Bush Tea Canal, his legs bound tight by the weeds. Unable to call out.

A tongue-tied death.

He wanted to say something to Mrs Baines, but he wasn't supposed to talk bad. But how else could he tell Mrs Baines that he loved Mikey?

Mrs Baines was not crying. There was sweat on her forehead and she was shivering. The fire in the grate wasn't lit. A paraffin heater in the corner of the room was churning black smoke.

Long before the end of the evening Mr Baines was no longer there.

Ingrid sat on a chair by the coffin. 'Alright, Lorne?' she said. Then her mousey head flopped to her shaking chest. Once, Ingrid had said that she'd seen a ghost at the end of her bed. A man in a black cape staring at her in the night.

Lorne felt sure that he would see Mikey's duppy. He and Tutus had seen duppies the day they'd moved into their house.

They'd been playing in the yard. They weren't supposed to go inside the shed, but they did. There was old furniture stacked against the wall. He and Tutus saw an old man and woman sitting in two dusty rocking chairs. Wizened old people with skin like tracing paper, looking with wonder at the bangarang of their life.

Tutus's eyes had been wide but calm, as if she'd seen duppies before. He'd felt darkness spreading around them. Smelt soil that had been shifted and turned, and the damp chalky smell of the walls. He remembered feeling scared for Tutus as he'd looked into her dark, wide eyes.

Poppa-Miller had gathered the old furniture that night, lit a fire in the yard, leaned against the plum tree and rolled tobacco. Smoke floated above his lips as, talking bad, he sent the ghosts on their way.

Lorne sneaked out of the Baines' house. The words in the room were soft and damp and he was starting to shiver too. He went down to Bush Tea Canal. It was grey, dark and drizzling.

He kneeled and put his face close to the dark water. It smelt piss-pot renk.

'Gwaan, Mikey,' he said.

SWINGING LOW

Southall, 1972

I remember the day Marisa arrived. It was during the big freeze of the 1960s. Snow everywhere.

She was thirteen, but she'd flown alone, thousands of miles on a jumbo jet, through dusk, dawn and turbulence, the wildness of Roaring River village – mangroves and scarp – still in her.

She was standing in the back room next to the wooden radiogram. Eyes wild; mouth screwed shut. She wore a yellow midi dress with a rounded wing collar, and a long cord of black obsidian hanging on her chest. Muma-Miller lined me up with the other children – the four-year-old twins, Agatha and Albertine, and Lorne. She pushed me forward. 'Gwaan Tutus, say hello to Marisa.'

I said hello and Marisa nodded at me and the other children, but she didn't speak.

Muma and Poppa-Miller had left Marisa in Jamaica when they came to England, when she was three years old.

There'd been a particular day when the subject of Marisa was raised. I was ramping with the other children in the dimly lit hallway. The ticky-tacky smell of beeswax was everywhere and Muma-Miller was on her hands and knees, bumping down the stairway, poking at pockets of dust. Her voice soulful-sad, crooned 'Swing low, swe-eet char-i-o-o-t comin' for to carry meee home.'

Muma-Miller reached the bottom of the stairs, rose and strode down the passageway to the cellar door. The cellar was a place of sawdust and splinters where Poppa-Miller spent his evenings cutting and hammering – maybe remembering the days when he used to cut cane on the plantation in Roaring River.

Muma-Miller wrenched the door open and bellowed, 'Massah, we leave the child when she wus three! Time movin' on. When we goin' send for her?'

Poppa-Miller's saw sliced back and forth. Then his gritty voice: 'Woman, where de money comin' from? Flights expensive. Money don't grow 'pon tree.'

Muma-Miller stamped her foot and shouted, 'Massah, you mus' think children grow 'pon tree.'

That first night, Muma-Miller told Marisa that she could cotch with Aunt Ermeldine who had a room downstairs. Muma-Miller spoke with a note of desperation – as if she were offering Marisa all the plumped-up warmth of the ten lost years.

Marisa's lips were thick and red, and there was a large mole, like a full stop, at the corner of her mouth.

'Me not sharing with no more obeah woman,' Marisa replied.

So Marisa squeezed into the sagging double bed – Agatha, Albertine and Lorne at the top, me and Marisa at the foot.

Marisa gave up her sulky silence; told us about the duppy-spirits that swung low above the swell of Roaring River. 'Yuh see when night-time come! Hell-fire! Nuttin' but Coolie duppies, Indians who used to bruck them backs on cane fields.'

She said the Indian spirits flew low over the fields of cane, looking for the secret land-passages of ice, now hidden beneath the sea, searching for their way home.

The way she told the story, with the window rattling against its rotting frame, was frightening and I moved closer to her. Marisa's body was cold.

'Them coolie duppies wus just appearing and disappearing, floating like them separate from the world,' she said.

One morning, several months later, Muma-Miller came into our room as we were getting ready for school. 'No school today,' she shouted as, one by one, she took our faces in her hands and slapped and smeared them with Vaseline. 'Lord, what a-something come down 'pon us, Jesus in His Mercy!' she cried.

Uncle Carlton came in his white Zephyr and we were herded into the ca and stacked onto the rigid laps of Muma-Miller and Aunt Ermeldine. Poppa-Miller sat up front.

'Me not sorry,' Marisa said, as she got in the car. 'Who she think she is? Tellin' me 'bout bad English.'

Marisa was in trouble at school. Again.

'Marisa, tell me, what did happen?' Muma-Miller said. 'Me have to have it clear inna me head for these law people.'

Marisa told us what happened between her and the teacher at school.

'The woman tell me to speak English,' Marisa said. 'What kinda language she think me speakin' if it not English?'

The teacher had stepped up to Marisa, so she'd thrown a chair at her.

Uncle Carlton drove us to the juvenile court, to the shrill lamentations of Muma-Miller: 'Jesus in Heaven come down from yuh throne and deliver me from dis tribulation.'

The Court House was a grey stone colonial building. We walked into the court room's drowsy murmurings and subdued coughs, and sat on the hard, wooden benches.

Poppa-Miller shifted his heavy frame again and again, his powerful hands weighted at his sides like mallets.

Marisa was beside me. Love, hate, hurt tied her tongue in a knot that she couldn't undo.

I put my hand in hers.

A woman in a tweed suit stood up and said that Marisa was a delinquent. 'There are certain principles accepted by my profession, and we will do everything to preserve the personal relationship between child and family.'

They came the following week. A small man, buttoned up in a black trench coat. A woman with thick calves and a doughy neck.

Poppa-Miller stayed in the cellar.

I watched from the top of the stairs.

'Marisa, you must come with us,' the woman said.

Marisa sucked air and circulated it around the tip of her tongue: 'Tcheeeww! Me not going!'

Muma-Miller made a nervous move towards Marisa. 'Gwaan, child, everyt'ing will be alright,' she said.

Marisa dodged Muma-Miller, but the woman and man took hold of her.

They pulled Marisa away.

Marisa's escape was reported in the local Gazette: 'Runaway taken back to Court.'

Marisa must have used all her creative abilities for flight. Dipping low amongst the summer workers as they flowed into the city. A fluttering cotton dress appearing and disappearing amongst the crowds.

Marisa didn't make it as far as our home – maybe she didn't intend to.

The police found her living with a Sikh family three miles away from us. The newspaper said it was a wonder how a delinquent child reached as far as she did without money, food or water.

The Sikhs had taken her in, fed her channa masala and rasmalai, put her in a bed of blue Indian cotton sheets with their four daughters.

Mohinda Singh, the father, said, 'It is our custom to give alms, when there is need.'

'Me not going back,' Marisa screamed when she stood before the court again. 'Me not going back to that mowly school. Me not tekking no more from that dutty headmaster.'

The Court never understood what she was trying to say about the things the headmaster had been doing to the girls in his care.

★

Winters are not as harsh as they were all those years ago. The snow falls like slushy cotton.

I visit Muma-Miller every week and it was on one of those visits that she showed me the letter from Marisa.

We were sitting in the kitchen, the old boiler clanking as we drank ginger tea. On the Formica table was the air-mail envelope, flimsy as blue Lignum Vitae – too light for the weight of its recriminations.

We hadn't heard from Marisa in twenty years, not since the day she left that boarding school.

Muma-Miller put on her glasses and squinted. She was sixty-eight – all collarbone, ruched skin and floral print housecoat. She shook as she read the letter.

Muma-Miller,
I was just a child when you left me in Roaring River with Ms Rosalita. You said you wos coming back. Every evening me look for you. Me see de women going home from the cane fields to them pickney.

Ms Rosalita said you never sent a penny for me. She mek me sleep in the buttery on the ashes.

At nights me cross the river to the old plantation and sleep on the wooden cots where the coolies dem did sleep. You shoulda left me in Roaring River and not bring me here.

Muma-Miller could not read the rest. Four pages of angry words indented through to the other side of the page. She put the letter face down.

Muma-Miller didn't say a word. No cries to Jesus in heaven. She could not call out to Poppa-Miller. His cellar was silent, the sawdust settled. He'd died two years ago.

She went to the larder and pulled down the biscuit

tin that contained her papers. She showed me the yellowing postal-order stubs. Every week, for eight years, Muma-Miller had sent Ms Rosalita ten shillings for Marisa's keep.

'I never forget my child. Never,' Muma-Miller cried. 'Lord, I never want to leave her, but Poppa-Miller said England was tough. Him say we couldn't mek it with a child. Plenty people did the same.'

Her cheekbones sunk into her face, pulling the pain deeper into her eyes.

I inhaled ice-cold air and gasped, wanting to rise up and leave. Wanting to find Marisa.

I looked at the snowflakes clinging to the window, then melting away.

SURVIVAL OF THE FITTEST

Southall, 1973

The rush of cold air woke me. Stale paraffin smoke braided the darkness.

The window was open, swinging.

Agatha was sleeping next to me. Lorne was a broken shape at the bottom of the bed. Albertine was missing.

I got up and went to the window. Swampy black clouds. The moon balanced on the spire of the church-shed in the back yard. Albertine was standing on the slanting slate roof, flannelette nightie fluttering in the wind.

Her eyes were open and she was staring ahead. Then the voice: 'Your name's stabbing my heart, girl. Pour rum on it. It's pain.' This was coming from Albertine's mouth.

I ran back to the bed and woke Agatha, Albertine's twin.

'Tutus, what you doing?'

I pointed to the open window. Agatha got up and went to the window. She screamed like a jezebel. She had the lungs for it. They were the only well-developed part of her. She was the smaller twin, born not much bigger than a blood clot. The one who got less of the nutrients. Less of the good looks.

Poppa-Miller burst in wearing his grey vest and long johns. 'What in damnation going on with oonuh pickney?'

Agatha pointed to the window.

Poppa-Miller climbed onto the roof and reached for Albertine. He grabbed her swaying body with his banana-fingered hands.

She screamed and clawed at his face. She didn't seem to know him.

Muma-Miller came running. She had a white cloth wrapped around her plaited head. She took one look at Poppa-Miller and shouted, 'Yuh blasted jackass. What if the pickney did drop? You blasted yeggeh-yeggeh!'

She was a Christian so she couldn't swear, but we all knew what she meant.

Poppa-Miller raised his hand to show that he had a hold of his daughter. 'Look ya! The pickney not falling anywhere.'

The nights hadn't been the same since Marisa arrived. That was when Albertine had started talking like a duppy, her voice as deep as Poppa-Miller's.

Agatha started wetting the bed after that night. Muma-Miller jumped around in her tartan slippers, pulling the sheets off the bed. 'Enough, enough, enough! All this sleep-walking, bed-wetting foolishness. Two of you come from the same egg; two of you mekking trouble. I calling Pastor, and I don't care who and who in this house don't like it.'

Pastor Grossman was often called on by his congregation to cast out spirits. Spirits that made men sin. Spirits that made children talk to duppies.

Pastor Grossman was in the front room when we got home from school. He was sitting in the bat-winged armchair, smiling his yellow-toothed smile at us, saying, 'Ohhh-ohhh! Childrehnn, come-pfuh, come-pfhu,' with his frowsy preacher's breath.

I ran to the kitchen where Aunt Ermeldine was shut in with her frying chicken. Anything to get away from Pastor Grossman. Anything for a piece of chicken.

Aunt Ermeldine was humming to herself, her voice rising and falling in military-style staccato.

Standing on tiptoe, I could just about see the tips of the chicken wings. They still had one or two feathers – they hadn't given up on the idea of flight. They hadn't reckoned on Aunt Ermeldine.

She hustled the wings around in the pan and covered them with a lid. She had no intention of giving me any chicken.

Aunt Ermeldine wasn't a Christian. She believed in 'The Survival of the Fittest'.

I gave up waiting for chicken and went back to the front room.

Pastor Grossman was still praying, his trembling hand was on Albertine's head. She was kneeling at his feet. Pastor Grossman's hair was barbered within a millimetre of his scalp and buds of sweat sprouted between the stubble.

'And now we ask you, Almighty Father, to cast out Satan. Ohhhhh, yes!' Pastor's voice rose to a dizzying descant. His eyes rolled in their sockets as his hands continued to shake Albertine's head, as if he was trying to shake the devil out of his hiding place.

Aunt Ermeldine came and hovered in the doorway.

Her maroon-brown face had soaked up the spitting chicken fat and the pores of her face were open.

Pastor Grossman released Albertine and reclined in the armchair with a sigh. 'Aiieeee. I don't know; I just don't know. Some kind of interference. The devil trying to get in between me and the Lord.' He looked at Aunt Ermeldine.

'A healer indeed,' said Aunt Ermeldine under her breath.

'Oh-oh, good lady, come join us in prayer; it's not too late to save your soul,' Pastor Grossman said.

'Save it, Pastor,' Aunt Ermeldine replied. 'Yuh come to me; mek me show yuh what healing is all about. Me mekking chicken wings with yam and dasheen. That's what you need. And as for Albertine, she just need some yard herbs and obeah.'

Muma-Miller got up from her knees. 'Oh God, everything spoil now.'

Pastor Grossman ate the yams and dasheen. He ate until the sweat poured from his scalp, down his neck, into his shirt collar. He mopped his face and ate. He belched a smelly preacher-breath smell and left.

That night Albertine woke screaming. She screamed, she thrashed. She said Marisa's ghost was in the church-shed.

Muma-Miller resorted to Aunt Ermeldine's herbs. Albertine stopped talking and walking in her sleep. Instead, she slept in her waking life. She went around all day, dazed, with a secret, serene smile.

Dust collected in the corners of Marisa's empty drawer. Spiders hung, timeless, their webs in the corners of the room. I willed myself to join Marisa's flight, but I hadn't found the way outside of my body.

One night, I went to Aunt Ermeldine's room when the others were asleep. She was straightening her hair, running the hot comb from scalp to short, rust-coloured ends.

'I want magic, too,' I said.

'Child, you should be in your bed.' She tacked in a hair grip to the stretch of hair that had been straightened and put the hot comb on the ironing board. She rubbed no-lye hair-grease into her palms and held her hands out to me. 'Empty,' she said. 'All gone. Bamboo dust. Chopped hair from the tail of a horse. That Pastor, I know what him doing.'

She lifted me up onto the chair and opened the window. 'You want to be a little obeah queen, huh?'

'I want to bring them all back,' I said.

'Here you been all this time, wanting to know, eh? Wanting to search, too.'

We set up a watch through the long night. Watching the dark sky above the spire of the shed in the back yard. Waiting. Listening.

Aunt Ermeldine, hummed her spell:

Hand a' bowl, knife a' throat...

In the morning I found myself asleep in the bed with the others. Albertine screamed in her sleep again. Convinced that Marisa's duppy had thrown heat on her, she stopped eating, and hovered on the patch of grass in front of the church-shed, cringing and watching.

Muma-Miller said Marisa wasn't dead, but she cried and wailed as she said it.

One Saturday, when Muma-Miller was at the market, Aunt Ermeldine buried a skeleton behind the church-shed next to the upturned church bell that was filled with rainwater and tadpoles. A small cluster of white bones, wrapped in blue cotton.

'What is it?' Albertine asked.

Lorne sniggered. 'Is a cat, or something.'

Aunt Ermeldine scattered something over the wet earth. 'We will be free now,' she said.

Albertine was at peace with the voices that spoke to her day and night. Nothing stopped the flow of words. Not the drugs, not the confinement of the mental home that finally took her.

On one of my visits to Muma-Miller, years later, she told me about the third child – the one that had died when Albertine and Agatha were born.

'That must have been Albertine's identical twin – they must have come from the same egg,' Muma-Miller said. 'Out of one egg, too many pickney. Too many minds.'

ROARING RIVER PICKNEY

Southall, 1979

Sunday, late afternoon, and we're sitting in front of the gas fire – me, Muma and my younger sister, Riley. Gas metre's guzzling the coins. Fire's sucking the moisture outta our bodies as we're stretched out on the purple fake-fur rug, drinking Muma's cure-all fish tea.

I say to Muma, 'I remember Baba-Lulla bathing me in Roaring River one morning when the water was cold and clear.'

Muma looks up from her magazine, lips cussed-up curly. 'Cheeeww! Tutus, stop yuh foolishness. Ain't no way yuh remember no such thing,' she says. 'Yuh was jus' a baby when we left my poopa and come to England. Yuh sat on my lap in the plane and doo-doo'd your nappies. That's how much of a baby yuh was! Left my yard in Roaring River for shantytown Southall. Bet yuh don't remember the cold-arsed blizzard when we got off the plane. Eh?'

'No, yuh don't,' Muma answered for me. 'This yah town full of washed-out people who stepped off dem planes and couldn't mek it to the bright lights. Me couldn't drag me backside no further 'cos me was carrying yuh!'

I respected the way Muma could ignite that kinda fire with two breaths. She seemed warmer for it at least.

Muma's memories were mash-up – burdened with me? She'd left me with Muma-Miller and Poppa-Miller for eight years where I ramped with their children, Lorne, Agatha and Albertine until Muma wanted me back.

Baba-Lulla once wrote to me saying that water had memory. He said I was a Roaring River pickney – the water memories were in me and that I must return one day.

'The rum musta killed my poopa by now,' Muma said.

The flames flickered and petered out.

Muma shouted, 'G'lang to yuh beds. This country cold and me nuh have money to burn.'

It was still light outside. On the dead-end street the noises of children ramping; men messing with cars; women's mouths flying.

Riley pleaded with her nostrils – one flared wide, wider, widest; the other squinched shut.

'Shut yuh nose hole,' Muma shouted. 'Yuh pickney think me have money coming outta my arse to feed that meter. Gwaan!'

We clomped upstairs to the damp bedroom; lino peeling like empty sweetie paper; the copper water tank in the airing cupboard hissing.

I lit the paraffin heater and went to bed with my schoolbook, *The History of Cristobal Colon*. Riley curled behind me, heavy vex-breathing.

I looked at the pictures of Cristobal Colon and his

sailors arriving at Discovery Bay. They carried gifts of blue glass beads for the Tainos who came to greet them in straw skirts.

The room darkened with the night and the paraffin flame flickered charcoal figures onto the wall.

He arrived that spring. A straight-haired, yellow-skinned Jamaican, wearing a blue velvet jacket and crimson flares.

I didn't trust his sour-grape green eyes and psyche-delic colours.

He held out a family-sized box of chocolates and a pink doll with blinking blue eyes.

'Call me Uncle Ransford.' He crouched down, face-to-face with Riley.

Riley took the chocolates but not the doll. 'We don't ramp,' she said.

I wanted to remind Muma that things never went well with uncles – especially the fenkeh-fenkeh ones with gifts. But she was already pumping the meter with coins.

By summer, Uncle Ransford's snakeskin boots were lined up under the stairs.

Come winter and all his records – *me very soul*, he said – were stacked on the MFI cupboard.

Cowboy music, Riley called them.

Trouble started for real the next winter. We were eating dinner at the Formica table.

'Ransford, yuh can fix that water tank soon?' Muma said. 'It still over-heating and water leaking 'pon de sheets and towels. The heap of noise the thing making in the night sound like duppy in the house.'

'Woman, I will tek care of it when me good and

ready. Me done tell yuh, is a simple thing to clear out the sediment, after all.' He stabbed a piece of cho-cho with his fork. Red shapes, like islands on a map, flushed across his cheeks.

Muma dished out the dessert. She'd gone as far as making puddings, always egg custard – a curdling corruption of the idea.

Ransford shovelled up the yellow mess.

Later, when we were in bed, we heard the *buudup-buuduuup* against their bedroom wall and the floor. Muma didn't shout, cry or cuss. I was vex about that. Afraid of what her silence would do to us.

Riley and me didn't talk much. Didn't need to – we dreamt in the same air space. But Riley started with the Lord's Prayer.

Deliver us from Evil. I watched Riley's breath in the bitter-cold room.

The water in the tank clanked like something was trying to get out.

Late in the night, when the noise in Muma's bedroom had stopped, I checked the tank. It was steaming hot and water was leaking onto the floor. I bandaged it with the white sheets. Listened to the clanking, tied the sheets tighter.

The next morning, Saturday, Ransford cotched down by the stereo listening hard to some cowboy singing, begging for cool water. He had a poor-thing look on his red face.

Muma's lips were swollen and she had a black eye.

Me and Riley were polishing the fireplace.

'Woman, you must stop the nag-nagging. Nagging bad for a man's soul. Me give yuh everything me have. Me heart and soul. Nuh true?'

Muma squirted the TV screen with Mr Sheen.

'God bun me if me lying,' Ransford called out.

Riley belched. She looked heavenward, 'Beg yuh pardon!'

Ransford stopped eating at the table with us.

Muma brought the tray to him where he sat on the sofa watching cowboy films on the telly.

'Pigs tails, woman? Is this yuh feeding me?' He didn't call her Ruby any more. 'This kinda cheap meat not good for a man's soul,' he said. 'Cheap cuts will fuck yuh up. I need steak, salmon, cutlets. What kind of a man yuh think yuh dealing with? Me not one of dem bush-bwoy from yard. A man like me needs *style!*'

I looked up at the ceiling where water from the tank was spreading in a dark patch.

'Ransford, I can't afford them kinda meats,' Muma said. 'Yuh said yuh was gonna leave money.'

Ransford stood up and spun the tray across the room where it hit the wall. He dragged Muma out of the room, up the stairs.

Me and Riley listened to the buff-buff-buff coming from the ceiling.

By the time Muma told us she was pregnant, Uncle Ransford and his cowboy music were gone. The week after he left, Muma burned with a fever for days. Then Riley caught it. I was afraid that our souls were burning.

I saw Ransford one Saturday afternoon inside the Railway Tavern with a white woman with gold hoop earrings the size of handcuffs.

When I told Muma, her mouth twisted-up like rope.

Ransford, the great red hope, was gone. Not white, but pale enough to drink the cool, clear water that would nourish his soul.

Lying in bed, reading and thinking about the child that's gonna come. My schoolbook says the Atlantic Ocean is thirty-three feet wider than when Cristobal Colon crossed it. More water everywhere.

The water tank rattles louder and hotter than ever. Me and Riley pad it up every night but the ceiling is sodden.

Riley didn't say The Lord's Prayer. She started singing the cowboy song, praying for cool water.

IN THE SPIRIT

Southall, 1979

They're always dressed in white, writhing like ghosts. Acting out, like that woman on the stage, head thrown back, words flying out her mouth. It gives Pastor the chance to wipe away the sweat on his temples. Then he's keying up the congregation to his pitch, shouting about the slackness and sinning of young people.

Why is he looking at her? Tutus thinks. This is the last time, the last raaatid time she comes. She can do better than this, even on a Sunday evening in a slum town. She tells herself that she only comes to be close to her grandmother, Muma-Miller, who is standing next to her, beating time with her tambourine, singing like her life depends on it.

But these people say they've got the key to the afterlife, and Tutus is open to anything that will provide a little stability.

Lloyd looks like he's just stepped outta the afterlife. He's at the end of her pew, standing like ancient boyman, brown-skinned, inlaid black eyes.

She turns and smiles at him. His pink water-mouth

doesn't smile back but there's a small movement in his eyes. Or maybe it's just the flickr-flickr-flickr from the strip fluorescent light high above him.

'There is no time to lose,' Pastor calls out. 'Come lay your head at the feet of God before judgement day; I will save you from the devil.'

The sistren on stage jump and stomp, their crimpelene-upholstered bosoms bouncing; their arms open wide for Tutus.

Tutus' face is hot with the heat coming from the electric fires that are in all the corners, hot as hell and probably a fire hazard in the clapped-out clapboard church.

Hellfire, she thinks, that's the place everyone thinks Lloyd is destined for. She's heard what the congregation say: 'The devil inside that bwoy.' 'Why him don't speak or smile or look people in the eye?' 'Him head not good.'

All Lloyd has to do to buy his place in the afterlife, is walk to the pulpit, kneel on the red cushions, at the feet of Pastor Grossman.

Tutus doesn't know why Lloyd comes, week after week. Arriving a little after the evening service, leaving just before the fire and brimstone sermon ends, and mostly managing to avoid having his face pulled to the stale bodies of the sistren, who have been jumping, singing and praising all day, leaving white halos around their mouths.

Tutus knows that the morning service has opened her up; she can feel the buzzing in her eyes, the light fizzing in her ears. And now the evening service, and everyone is high on the strange Sunday darkness, the quiet that mingles with the singing and praying.

Tutus listens as Pastor's voice recedes and she hears the banging of his fist on the pulpit, louder, louder – a steady beating drum. The electricity in her ears buzzes, becomes a cool breeze, becomes a whisper: he is not to be trusted.

A chair scrapes against the wooden floor and Tutus turns around.

Lloyd has stepped into the aisle, facing the altar head-on.

'The devil is waiting for you this yah night,' Pastor bellows. 'Don't let him catch you.'

Lloyd stands there, swaying a little in his two-tone suit.

Muma-Miller is warbling like a trapped bird.

Something about Lloyd doesn't look right – he's smiling, but it doesn't look like his smile; it looks like the smile of two people, pulling in opposite directions.

Sister Levy goes to him, takes his arm, tries to pull him up the aisle, but his feet aren't moving.

Black rain at the window. The air smells of damp cellulite and bad-belly belches. Tutus wants to run.

Lloyd's eyes open wide and he starts laughing in a deep baritone that's not like the voice of a young man – more like that of a sixty-year-old.

He's in the spirit, Tutus thinks. But she still doesn't know who is not to be trusted. Lloyd? Pastor?

Lloyd falls hard.

The singing stops.

Lloyd's body is twitching and jerking.

'Ah de Devil!' a man shouts. They scramble around him, keeping a safe distance.

Pastor steps into the circle, put his hand on Lloyd's head, holds it there.

'Let him go!' Tutus shouts. But they ignore her. Maybe she hasn't shouted; maybe it's just in her head. She starts to sing, to cool the fire in her throat, to see what she can summon. It's not a hymn; it's a dub track from last night's raving – a rootsy chanting that's full of Kumina. Tutus keeps on singing, trying to drown out Pastor's praying.

The fluorescent light flickers several times.

Lloyd has stopped twitching; he's completely still.

The fluorescent light goes out, leaving them all in cave-dwellers' darkness.

GWAAN

Southall, 1983

No tap dancing or any shit like that. Riley wanted to dance – the kinda moves where you kick your leg up inna your face, your arms spread out like the wings of a plane. But she was marooned on the fake fur rug with her family, in front of the gas fire. Her Muma's legs were opened around the chipped wooden tray of mugs. Jets of druggy, purple gas pump-pumping from the fire.

The women dancers on TV looked foolish in their frou-frou clothes, twirling and prancing. Riley jumped up and stepped towards the glass cabinet.

They looked up at her – Crimpey, her little brother, Tutus her older sister, and her Muma – their gold-brown, red-brown and cocoa-brown faces glistening, their mouths split open in expectation.

'Dance yuh magic, but mind the cabinet,' her Muma said, like she always did.

Riley was twelve years old but she knew how to shay-shay, flex and vibrate her little arse. Improvise to guitar riff, drum lick and saxophone spray. She didn't skin-up at anything. Not even her poopa. She took his licks like everyone. Only she never bawled.

Muma had lit the paraffin heater, but the house was still cold n'raas. The paraffin heater gave out as much heat as a spliff. Riley knew all about spliffs; after school she got charged on ganja with the rude-bwoys from the cemetery side of the estate. Cotched-up in one of the garages, sitting on boxes, inhaling until their chests inflated like skeletons coming back to life.

'Do a spin, Riley,' her little brother shouted. 'Spin fast, like you did last time.'

Riley looked down on her family. She turned and stood with her back to them, facing the cabinet. It was the only pretty thing in the house: white-lacquered concertina doors painted with dancing geishas; a sliding glass cabinet at the bottom that was filled with china for special occasions.

Special occasions never came.

Muma pulled the blanket over the children. Gave them mugs of boiled ganja tea mixed with white rum. Later, she'd dash it into the corner of the rooms to keep evil spirits away. But Poopa always came back.

Riley spun and faced her family. There was a look in her Muma's eyes that made Riley's heart hurt bad-bad-bad. Muma's eyes had stopped speaking.

Riley walked to the darkened back of the room where damp clothes were hanging on the clothes rail.

'Gwaan, Riley,' her sister shouted.

Her little brother looked afraid. He'd seen the other side of her.

Riley relaxed until her body was as limp as the damp clothes; she hunched her shoulders so that it looked like she was hanging by her shoulders. She triggered her waistline and spine. Again and again, until it seemed that a strange body was moving through her.

Muma said nothing. Her pretty-pretty lips were swollen with bitter pride and humiliation.

That night, Riley opened the bedroom window, looked down into the street and beyond the estate.

She climbed out the window and jumped onto the top of the front door porch. She squatted and looked up into the sky. It was vex-black and spitting stars.

She raised her arms above her head, inhaled and jumped. Legs split wide, arms high. A star.

A falling star.

★

Forty years on and Riley was cotching in Club Couture – a dry little wine bar on the high street. Deggeh-deggeh wine, bling furniture, old-timers. Music that took you way back.

She was looking up at the cabinet-sized plasma screen above the bar. Another raaatid pop-star contest. A bumpy-faced bwoy in skinny jeans and baseball cap was rapping and bucking. Sweat on his face. Doubled up, straining on a note for so long it was a wonder he didn't fart.

'You're really current, bang on-trend,' the judge said. She was glossy, all cho-cho green eyes, dasheen dark lips stretching from one gold-weighted earlobe to the other. 'You've got something. We wanna see more of you; see what else you can do,' she said.

Riley imagined herself on that stage, in an arena with 90,000 people, showing everybody what she could do. A DJ would put on a bruck-neck track and she'd throw down her moves.

But she wasn't on stage. She worked in an old people's home, just like her Muma had. She looked around the bar. Grizzly men wearing moccasins, old Gabiccis and bombo bling.

Walkman came across to her and slammed down a brandy and coke, slipped something into her hand, whispered in her ear, walked back to the pool table with his stix-man swagger.

'Yeah, nice-nice,' she said. She liked hard-backed men like that. Hair plaited tight on his scalp. Eyeballs dipping below the eye rim.

Just like her poopa.

She went down the greasy stairway to the toilet, into the green cubicle and snorted a line of coke.

She heard her Muma's voice that winter evening all those years ago. 'Gwaan, Riley. Gwaan, nuh. Dance the magic for us. Dance it!'

'Nah, man, it's time to leave all that alone now. It doesn't do any good,' Riley said. 'No more raatid dancing. There ain't no magic.'

She went up to the cabinet and slammed her fist hard against the lacquered top.

The glass doors rattled.

Her muma screamed.

'I ain't doing this stupidness anymore. Chah!'

Her younger brother watched her. She knew he was afraid of her. Sometimes, when Muma was at the night-shift in the old people's home, she'd get him ready for bed, pull his jumper over his head and hold it around his face for a while.

'Get it off, get it off,' he'd cry. 'I can't breathe.' Then he'd scream, get hysterical. When he'd screamed long enough she'd take it off and hold him close, kissing his cornmeal-coloured face, rubbing his scalp until he fell asleep.

She needed him to scream for her.

Riley went upstairs, back to the bar. The audience on TV were shouting and screaming for another singer. His maaga body flexing, brucking out robot moves – head and neck on the left, torso on the right, his legs somewhere in the middle.

Bombo!

Riley's body was heating up, her legs trembling. She slipped off the stool onto the floor. The tiled floor was cool. She got up, went over to the raised dance-floor where, in the evenings, vex couples danced to lovers' rock.

Riley started to flex and vibrate her not-so-little arse.

She couldn't kick her legs up in her face. She put her arms out like a plane. The room tilted. She was dancing with geishas. They were bowing to her. She could hear her grandfather's drums. She could see Roaring River.

She jumped.

OLD TIME PEOPLE

London, 1995

'Me ah obeah man,' the old man said, his voice dry and slow as the drag of goat skin on red earth.

I told him my name was Tutus.

'Missus, me can travel through night,' he said. 'From country to country. All you would see is likkle light coming from me body. Like firefly.'

He was leaning against the bus stand wearing a trilby and a black double-breasted jacket winched at the waist by a leather belt. A maaga bundle of frayed rag and shallow breath.

It was seven-thirty on Saturday morning. I'd left everyone at the shebeen after a night of raving. I was charged on blow-backs of weed and dub. I could see that he was from the tribe of Old Time People.

Like Muma-Miller.

I'd left Southall, Muma-Miller, Poppa-Miller, Muma and the children, twenty years ago. Moving further and further away. Trying to escape the dark-room life where everything was colourless and un-formed.

The old man looked at me, tilted his head. 'Is which island yuh from?'

His nostrils were wide, but he was struggling to breathe. His ribs moved beneath the jacket like an old accordion.

'My people are from Jamaica. Roaring River,' I said. 'D'you know it?'

'Mmm, mek me see… Yuh people still there?'

'My grandfather – we don't know whether he's still alive.'

'Look 'bout. Everybody is duppy.'

His patois was raw. I heard my own voice – a mix of repetitive receptionist greeting and hyped secretary.

'Well sah! If yuh say you born there, then yuh know about obeah. What it can do. If this life is haunting you, I can drive it out. Drive you onwards.' He pushed himself up and stepped towards me. The movement stirred the smell of his unwashed body.

I stepped away from him.

Two Somalian refugee women walked past in long veils and robes the colour of turmeric. They had shadows under their eyes, their skin dry as caked mud. There was blood-red henna on their hands.

'Them is duppy,' he said. 'No blood inside them.'

Lights went on in the pound shop. Indian men were putting crates of yard food and fruit out in front of their shops. Inside, a butcher was chopping into bony goat meat with a large meat knife. There was dried blood on his apron. Everything was in colour except the Old Time Man – and me.

'Yuh been away from your land too-too long,' he said. 'Listen, nuh, I flash back to the homeland when-ever I want. Cos me is obeah man. Back to the Bamboo foothills that reach way down to the Rio Grande. The light on the headland – bwoy, that light. That light!'

He threw up his eyes to the sky and held his pose.

The bus wheezed in and the black concertina doors opened. I stood aside for him to get on the bus. I didn't want him walking behind me.

He shook his head. 'I'm still waiting.'

'But this is the only bus that stops here.'

'I'm still waiting,' he said again. 'Me no need no bus.'

Something about the turn of his mouth, the stare, the stance, the light coming from his eyes – I was charged enough to believe that maybe he was an obeah man.

'Your waiting is over. You should go. G'lang, Missus.'

I got on the bus and left him there. Sunlight popping all around him.

Many months later, in early November, I saw the other one. An early chill had drawn an artful dusting of frost across pavements, roofs and windows. Everything had a grainy, blurred quality. I was on the bus to Victoria, wrapped in a sheepskin coat. The bus stopped next to a line of people huddled beneath a bus shelter. I noticed her straight away. She was bent forward, scooped out of her hips by some spinal degeneration. She wore a battered coat that had perhaps once been brown or red. It hung around her hunched back like a saddle blanket.

She stepped onto the bus, bringing the smell of grave dust and rotting flesh. 'Whe' de bus going?' she asked the driver. Her voice was determined, dry.

'Victoria, love, it's going to Victoria,' the bus driver said. 'Now come through, you're blocking the way. Come on now.'

'No, sah, not far enough.' A buoyant mass of woolly grey hair shook like a chemical explosion.

Muma-Miller would never have gone on the street looking like that. The old woman's feet were swollen and caked in dirt, clad in worn-down brocade slippers. Yet I knew that a long time ago she would have greased her skin, used a hair grip to poke wax from her ears, a sharp enamel comb to clean her flaking scalp. On Sundays she would have gone to a clapboard Church heated with paraffin lamps, to beat tambourines for the Lord. Or maybe she believed in something more powerful.

The bus driver shouted louder, 'Where d'you want to go, love?'

'You don't hear whe' me say! You not going far enough!' He shrugged his shoulders and shut the doors on her and she stepped back onto the street.

The bus carried on… *Ringgg-ringg-ringg*

Victoria…

…Queen's Park…

…New Cross…

That night I heard the sound of the ringing in my dreams. Go on, go on, it seemed to say.

I see the picture of Muma-Miller and Poppa-Miller. The one that was framed in thick glass above the fireplace at Lady Adelaide Road. The picture is floating just beneath the surface of Roaring River.

Muma-Miller is wearing a fairytale dress of pin-point shot taffeta. It is frothing light and she is smiling. A white handbag on her left arm. Poppa-Miller is beside her, wearing a tropical dinner coat and dress pants. Sharp creases and a boot-string moustache.

They are Old Time People: the old man, the old woman, Muma-Miller, Poppa-Miller. They are back in the photographer's studio, where all the Old Time People once went. Holding their poses against the false backdrop of opulence. For a moment they have it all: the plush furniture of the studio, their Sunday-best clothes.

The lens is aimed at them. There is a flash of light.

Their image sinks deeper into Roaring River.

THE OLD GOAT

Southall, 2001

The phlegm was on Poppa-Miller's chest, in his throat. He hacked up the little he could; spat it on the side of the pillow; hoped it would dry before the nurse came. A smoke of jackass-rope would bring the rest up from his lungs, but no one had the sense to bring any. As if it mattered what he did to his body now! He asked for rum and what did they give him? Blood!

There was a snap-snap of joints as he tried to sit up. His body was hungry for moisture, but those sources in his body were dried-up.

There were three others in the ward: two withered white men and a balding Asian lady who had propped herself up with all her shaking strength in an ugly chair. The men were on their backs, staring with moon-frosted eyes.

Poppa-Miller decided to stir them up. 'I dream me mother last night,' he said. 'She come, asking me why I been away so long – so-so long.'

One of the men moaned and turned on his side. His blanket shifted, exposing the gaping hospital gown.

Muma-Miller cleared her throat and patted her lap with a show of tenderness that she had not yet offered him. He had always turned his back on foolish feelings. But hell-fire! This was different, wasn't it? He looked at her, sitting in the chair beside his bed.

He thought of the things he had achieved in his eighty-three years: buying the house on Lady Adelaide Road – what a come-up from his bamboo shack. Even so, he liked to think the old shack was still there by Roaring River. He had built it to last – cutting part-ripe bamboo that would never rot but harden with age. He tied the frame with China-wis plastered with earth and wood-ashes; smoothed it with guinea grass and a tenderness of hand that he had never shown any woman.

'What's wrong?' Muma-Miller asked. He realised he had been grunting. He could not tell her that he wanted to die back in his shack – not after all the sacrifices they made to come to England. And judging by his colour, he was not sure he would make it back to Lady Adelaide Road, let alone to Roaring River. The African nurse who had shaved him that morning held a mirror up to his face, 'Here now, Mr Miller; see how much better you look after the transfusion.'

But he saw that his once brown face was now the dull-bronze colour of cane trash. When he came to England in the sixties, his skin had turned purple-black from the cold. Reverse tanning. He wondered what colour he would be when he was dead. Cho! He needed to get back to his bamboo shack. Quick-time. He twisted his hands and shook the plastic tubes that tethered him to the bed. He was tied up like the goat he had brought for the family's first Christmas in Lady Adelaide Road.

He brought the goat from Southall market for the

Christmas of 1966. He led the shaggy off-white, red-eyed animal down the Broadway past the Water Tower. The streets were busy with young people going to the Palace Cinema; cars and scooters zipping up and down the road. People stared, but he went on strolling, smoking Golden Virginia tobacco, pulling the reluctant animal along. He knew Muma-Miller would be vex. He went through the gate in the back yard, pushed open the kitchen door and told her to come look. She looked out the window and saw the goat. Then she was up in his face. 'But, man, where yuh going with that animal?'

'Is for Christmas,' he said. 'I want fresh goat-meat.'

She sucked her teeth. 'Look-yah, man, I have enough to do around this old house. Yuh just tormenting me.' But she just liked running up her mouth.

He killed the goat and she skinned, cleaned and cooked it on Christmas Eve.

The day after Boxing Day, a young, bumpy-faced inspector came knocking at the door. The inspector quoted this-and-that. Poppa-Miller asked the inspector how the hell was he supposed to know that in England you couldn't buy a goat and slaughter it for your own pot. But the inspector was still bleating.

'Look yah, sah, I gave the Indian man in the market good-good money for the goat,' said Poppa-Miller. But the inspector was not interested.

Poppa-Miller lost his temper: 'Look, bwoy, I gave the goat a clean cut.' He slid his thick hands against his throat to show the inspector. The inspector ran off.

'Nurse, I want to piss, Poppa-Miller shouted.' The nurse brought the pan and as he strained to squeeze out a few drops. He thought that at least Muma-Miller would not have to put up with his bush habits anymore: blowing his nose in her tea towels, pissing in the back yard on her tomatoes…

Poppa-Miller stirred on the hospital bed. He had fallen asleep, but he heard Muma-Miller saying:

'I don't know why those people bothered. Let him go in peace. Cho! Why give him someone else's blood. It's not the Lord's way. Oh-what-a-something.'

She was speaking stoosh – that high-pitched voice with the batty-broad vowels that she only used in public. All these years and what? Did she think he didn't know her? He knew how she felt about Baba-Lulla. That was why she had been so hard with him. That was why he had taken it. He didn't mind – he never wanted a love relationship. He tried to avoid it, even with his children. How would they have survived in England if they had come with their heads filled up with fool-fool ideas about love?

'Marisa,' he whispered. 'Where is my Marisa?'

A tray of food hovered over his bed. A pot of white yoghurt. They had given him the blood of some poor man; now they were feeding him baby food! He had given his blood to the Mother Country. Drip-fed it, oiled the machines of the factory with his sweat. Now it was pay-back time – blood and yoghurt!

Muma-Miller leaned over his tray and picked up the spoon. 'Come, nuh, man, eat little something.'

'Yes, I will eat, and let the worms enjoy it,' he said. He could feel them writhing around inside his gut, feasting on the new blood. 'I want to go back home.'

'Back home?'

'Roaring River.'

'But, Poppa-Miller, you don't have anybody there. You know that.'

She was right. All his family and friends from Roaring River were dead. He was not sorry that he had missed their funerals. All that play-acting: the falling down on knees, the tearing at hair, the beating of breasts. Would anyone do that for him? Would Muma-Miller make a show of trying to jump into his grave and go down with him? Would their son, Lorne, have to hold her back? No. He did not suppose she would.

Was it too late for a holiday back home to Roaring River? He had never taken a holiday in his life, but he'd always planned on going somewhere. He pictured himself in Roaring River, floating on his river reed mattress. He turned his face away from Muma-Miller and a warm light reflected from the window onto his face. The white bedside cabinet, the monitor, Muma-Miller, all faded into a clinical white blur. He closed his eyes and the light grew larger. He followed it as it expanded into a bright, shining distance.

He came to. Went back. Went somewhere altogether different. Saw himself floating down Roaring River, the ridiculous hospital gown spreading and floating around him. He was a water lily.

He floated until he came to his bamboo shack on a distant shore. There was a small fire outside. Somebody was inside his shack!

'Poppa-Miller, you alright?' He opened his eyes and saw Muma-Miller leaning over him.

'I not gone yet,' he told her. She sighed and sat back on the plastic orange chair. Mebbe now, he thought, would be a good time to ask God's forgiveness for sleeping with Aunt Ermeldine when Muma-Miller was at church; for cheating at dominoes. For leaving his little daughter, Marisa, in Roaring River. For not bringing her to Southall until she was too old to remember them. For letting those interfering government people take her away. He allowed himself the luxury of a few tears. It felt good. More phlegm came off his chest and he coughed and hacked.

One of the men in the ward was drooling as he tried to talk; the other was sleeping and his chest was rattling. Oh well, he thought, once a man, but twice a child. He, too, was like a child – tired, restless, wanting to live. He slumped against the pillow. He was coming… going… back in the hospital… back to the bright light…

He could see his wooden shack clearly now. He was young and fit again, wearing his calico shirt and crocus-bag trousers, walking through the thicket of bamboo. He went inside his shack.

Marisa was there, sitting on his river reed bed, eating coolie plums from a calabash. She looked up at him and held out the bowl.

'Come, Poopa, take a plum. I light the fire. I been waiting.'

THE OFFERING

Roaring River, 2002

Rio Cobre, Mount Diablo. Spirit light moving across mauve mountains and black rivers. Tutus wanted the blood-shot-eyed driver to go faster, blur the landscape. But he drove slowly once he left the city, pointing out landmarks with his thick fingers.

He pulled up at the ridge, insisting that she look down. She got out of the car and, with sleep still in her eyes, looked into the oval valley to where he was pointing.

'See deh! That town fenced in by cane and cockpit – pothole and scarp. Beautiful, but it dread, missus.' He pointed out the patchwork cane fields, the factory in the centre with dark coiling smoke, and the village beyond.

They drove on and when they came to Baba-Lulla's land she gathered up her bags and got out of the car. He took the money she gave him, and made a move to get out of the car.

'These are my people,' she said.

He looked in her face, shook his head, laughed and said, 'What a thing!'

She waited until he drove away before carrying her bags up the steep path to the house.

Baba-Lulla stood on the veranda, erect, attentive.

'Who's you?' He called out, his dead eyes scanning the air.

'Tutus,' she said.

He came down the steps, his footing steady.

He asked her again and again who she was.

She put her bags down and walked to him. His shoulder-length hair was still black, but sparse, and his body was as bony as a stalk of cane. She said her name once more, but he still didn't understand. She was afraid that she was too late.

He reached out and collected strands of her Indian hair, his fingers as restless as river reeds. 'Oh-ohhh – the Roaring River pickney come back!' He reached his arms out to the left and right side of her. 'Where is Ruby?'

'Mother couldn't come.'

He slumped onto the steps and wouldn't speak. She watched him, sitting there goggle-eyed as an owl, staring.

'Forty-something years now Ruby gone,' he said. 'But her spirit nevah leave this yah place. I feel it all 'bout. I need her here, to stop this haunting.' He moaned and cried a little and she put her arm around him. She felt his body trembling.

After a while, he led her onto the polished wood veranda that stretched along the length of the house. It was tidily set with table, chairs, river-reed mattresses, chulah and a blue rug with turquoise cushions.

She wanted to throw herself down on the rug, give herself up to the heat and light, but he took her bags into the house, brought out a tray of sorrel syrup, rotis and vegetables.

After they had eaten, she gave him her mother's offering. 'Grandfather, these are for you.'

He turned the four red-gold bangles around in his hands, feeling the shape, the small scratches. He clanked them together like cymbals. 'These things won't sweet me. Them not flesh.'

'They were your mother's bangles. Mother said you gave them to us when we left the island.'

He put the bangles on his wrist. 'Oh-oh, yes, yes, my muma's.' He shook his withered arm. 'Only the cane left to fight,' he shouted. 'That is what my muma said when she did mash-down her troubles, and, bwoy, what a way she would shake her maaga fist with these bangles.'

'Mother says to tell you…'

'But why she send these back to me?' he cried out. 'I mus' wait five hundred years for my only daughter to come back to me – in spirit, like a Taino?'

'She's going to try to come next year when things are better.'

'My poopa and muma cut cane and hacked yellow limestone – India nevah see them again.'

She followed him out onto the land. It was six o'clock. Bushes and trees were etched into the oncoming darkness like tribal markings.

'Where are we going?' she asked, but he wouldn't say.

He led her into the heart of a thicket of banana trees. 'Come, child, see them there.'

She stooped down and could just make out the cement-covered tombs with the names of her great-grandparents. Bright red buds sprouted around them like lanterns.

She could smell the deep, loamy soil.

'The cane sucked the life out of them,' Baba-Lulla said.

His voice faded, merged into the humming dark-ness. She felt homesick – not for any home she'd ever known. She put her hands out to the distant mountains that were now circled by mist.

Baba-Lulla turned to her and she saw the mist in his eyes.

Some of the villagers came up after dinner, having heard the news of her arrival from the taxi driver. They hugged and prodded her, some remembering her birth. Others talked about Ruby: young, beautiful, troubled by the man who'd left her when she was pregnant – a man she would never name.

Baba-Lulla played his tabla drums and the old people shay-shayed in the darkness until she could feel the night hot and cold with Taino spirits.

Baba-Lulla was seventy and blind, but the next morning, after breakfast, he said, 'Come yah.'

She followed him further up into the mountain as he cracked his machete against the bush, his dark face hollowed out with exertion. She was surprised at his energy. It was a hot morning and they stopped to rest in the shade of an overhanging rock. Baba-Lulla wiped his brow with a white rag and said, 'Big-men came, long time back. From some department or other, with their boasty bellies and some old-time map, looking for a Taino cave. Muma told them to mek haste and gwaan. She shouted at them, "You took our fingerprints. This is our land now." She shook her hands at them, with these same bangles.'

Further up, he cut through hanging roots and strangling vines that were webbed together. Cleared a way to a concealed boulder and slipway that had been covered by dense brush. At the entrance of the cave, he pushed her forward.

She switched on the torch he'd told her to bring, gasped at the volcanic artistry of the vaulted roofs. As a child she'd dreamed herself into Taino caves on many nights, seeking refuge from the concrete estate, bad-eyed uncles and the damp pebble-dashed house. She was here now.

Ants and spiders crawled black trails on the ground. She stepped through silt crusted with fossils of camelis, armadillos and manatees.

She pressed her head against the damp mucous walls. Gour pools, sinkholes and river passages gurgled and she looked again at the walls, saw the oval faces with sloping narrow eyes carved into the rock.

A small wooden zemi god on the floor, its white shell-eyes staring at her.

She remembered what Baba-Lulla had said to her on the way up: 'Them Tainos was trying to get back to that ice place them come from,' he said. 'Sometimes people do go back. They have no choice. No more haunting, my child. No more. You staying here, or you going back?'

The faces on the wall were staring at her, waiting for her answer.

Nesting cave swallows swooped up in the damp air. She switched off the torch.

ORCHIDS AND BONES

Roaring River, 2004

Tutus heard Osorio calling her. She went outside to the back of the house where he was on his hands and knees, his face close to the earth. He was a tubby man, his paunch netted in a too-small string vest, his eyes protruding like a just-caught fish. He helped her to grow the orchids that she sold to the hotels in Negril.

'Missus, look yah,' Osorio called. 'Ah mus' be goin' mad – we nevah plant these yah. I nevah see dem before.'

Tutus crouched down beside him. In the damp red earth were small clusters of orchids. They were six inches long, with carnelian eyes and red-purple veins in the throat.

Tutus put her nose to one of the orchids that had risen, unbidden, from the earth. It smelt of oranges and chalky river water. It smelt of Baba-Lulla.

She had lived here with Baba-Lulla – on his land, in the house his parents had plastered with earth and ash, in the mountains, one thousand feet above sea level, above the valley, above Roaring River. In a world of mutating mist and macca.

She had lived with Baba-Lulla for two years before he died. His last clear words to her before his delirium, *Yuh a Roaring River pickney. Stay 'pon the trail.*

He'd told her about Taino caves, rivers and secret trails.

She drove down the mountain on the narrow potholed road, the bush clawing at her small red car. In a trance she stared at the gold light swinging in the valley below; the car rocking and bouncing close to the edge. She thought of her long-ago life in England with Muma-Miller, Marisa, mother, Crimpey and Riley. Saw the broken lines of their faces forming and unforming in the light. Felt their heat in her bones.

When she came to Roaring River village she saw the empty black skins of diving suits and guide lines. Dinghies, breathing tanks and underwater lights cluttered the river bank. She had heard about the archaeologists, but the sight of the futuristic equipment on the shore made her feel that time was running out.

The mid afternoon light was darkening, the valley collecting red volcanic light that swirled and stirred.

The old women higglers – Estrianna, Lundie and Esmie – stood behind an area cordoned off with a rope, watching and waiting. Tutus felt sure that one of them would recognise the orchid, know its name. Know its story. The old women were lopsided. Tutus imagined their dimpled thighs sunken into decaying hipbones. She wondered how long their bones would carry them. She wondered what would become of their bones.

'Looks like they're here for a while,' Tutus said. 'Hope they find what they want and leave.'

Lundie patted her heart, as if sending it to sleep, then

shouted, 'Them not fooling me. Taino pots my back-foot! Dem people digging for gold!'

The women greeted Tutus with gummy indifference, not teasing her like they usually did. 'How many Englishman you did leave in England? Them was good as a back-a-yard man?'

Tutus showed them the orchid, but they were too concerned with the shard washers – women hired from the village – who moved with new-found importance, enamel basins balanced on their heads.

One of the archaeologists, who had been taking pictures of the river, came towards them. His black eyes were old as night. His nose was flat. Cheekbones high. So many lines, his face like a page of hieroglyphics.

He took the orchid, laid it flat in his palm. 'I don't know this beauty; we were in Venezuela last year. Saw beautiful Gongora in the lowlands. Nothing as beautiful as this.'

Lundie stepped in. 'Never mind 'bout flowers, bwoy, how long you people planning to stay 'round here, causing disturbance, eh? Fouling de river water with yuh dis and dat.'

'Professor Calabres is happy to speak with everyone to explain what we're doing to preserve the environment.' He pointed out a stooped, grey-haired man, and the matriarchs strode towards him.

The archaeologist said his name was Guarocco, Rocco for short; said he was a researcher at the Historical Archives of Santiago in the Dominican Republic. He said the on-land team had discovered kitchen middens and Taino shards. 'There was a Taino settlement here,' he said.

'The villagers could have told you that,' Tutus said.

He gave the orchid back. 'Maybe they can tell me about sacrificial sites and burial grounds. That's what I'm looking for – bones.

'You should talk to the old people. They can tell you the important things – what they want you to know.'

'And you?' He caught her eye, held it in the black pit of his for a second.

'I'll go see what your Professor has to say about protecting the river.' She walked away.

It was Orsorio who told her about the big discovery several weeks later. Fifteen skeletons in an underwater cavern of the river, along with a canoe. She went straight away.

Professor Calabres had set up a laboratory in the old sugar mill where the plantation had been. Tutus smelt the sweetness and decay.

'We'll be making announcements at the end of the week,' Professor Calabres said. 'We can't say anything now.' His eyes were brighter, his mouth wider. His body upright.

She found Rocco on the river bank.

'It was a burial ground,' he said as they sat down to drink the bottled water that was handed out. 'Proving it will be difficult.' He pointed out the silver air-balloons they were using to lift the finds to the surface. 'I managed to get some pictures of the skeletons,' he said.

Tutus knew that it was no burial ground. The Tainos had not intended their bones to lay there. They'd been looking for a secret trail, to escape the Spanish, hundreds of years ago. That's the story Baba-Lulla told her.

'Don't you think it's a sacred place, no matter how long their bones have lain there?' she asked.

'My parents took me to a museum in Spain when I was young,' Rocco said. 'There was a bronze statue of a Taino girl. The plaque said something elaborate, ironic. It said her name was Ycara. I'll never forget her name. Then, something like, *This woman has been brought to Spain from the New World to show the invincibility of her people.* I believe in invincibility. I dive for it. Maybe one day I will die for it.'

'The villagers don't like it.'

'You don't like it, but maybe your reasons are different. I have stories too. Let me tell you one. Tonight, here.'

She brought river-reed mattresses and laid them far from the cordoned area of the river. She and Rocco lay side-by-side, the black sky arched around them like a cave.

'Why are you so interested in Tainos?' she asked. 'Do you have Taino blood?'

'It's not all about the dead. If we find a burial site it'll bring a little money to the villagers.'

'Maybe they'd rather tell their own stories.'

'Look, there's the North Star,' he said.

'I prefer the small stars. The ones without names,' Tutus said.

'The Tainos navigated by the stars when they sailed on long journeys,' Rocco said. 'If food became scarce on one island, some of the Tainos would pack their possessions and migrate to another island. They'd pack cassava bread, dried turtle meat, gourds filled with mabi wine. On the day of departure, they'd eat soap-wood berries with their people – to sweeten the departure.'

He rolled closer, shaped himself around the side of her body. She felt his bones – hard and strange.

'Departures can't be sweetened,' she said.

She saw herself being taken away from Muma-Miller's house, over the bridge to the wasteland estate where she spent the rest of her childhood with Ruby and the 'uncles' that came and went. She remembered the day Marisa was taken away from them – the hurt a mineral pain lodged deep in her bones. The memory of Marisa's face, gone.

'A subterranean site is like a photograph,' Rocco said. 'Water preserves things for thousands of years.'

'Water has memory,' Tutus said.

'I'll remember that whenever I dive. It'll be my mantra.'

She couldn't feel his bones now, only the warmth of his blood as the air cooled. She turned on her side to face him and saw a face from a lost past, lined with the trails of many people. She ran her finger across the lines below his eyes.

Tutus told Rocco about her great-grandparents, the Lullas. How they sailed from India in 1906, built their lives and drowned their spirits in sugar cane. She told him how she came in search of Baba-Lulla.

'I stayed because I want to stop seeing ghosts.'

'I can't say that I see ghosts, but I feel the magic of the things I find.'

She moved away from him and sat up. 'I want magic too,' she said, in almost the same way she'd told Aunt Ermeldine, the obeah woman in their family, many years ago.

Much later, they fell asleep. Dreaming, she saw Rocco deep in the river, cut off from his guide line.

His body sinking to the bottom, to Coaybay – dwelling place of the dead.

She woke and looked at him. It looked as if the bones of his face had fused together, the lines of his face no longer symbols, but a sound. She looked in the distance to the part of the river that had been cordoned off and heard voices. The riverbank was cluttered with Taino canoes and Naje oars. There was a glint from a secret snakewood fire. On the shore, creeping up from the water, she saw the long-limbed orchids, the red-purple veins throbbing at their throats. Their carnelian eyes wide open.

SOFT TO THE TOUCH

Roaring River, 2007

Muma-Miller took the bus to Secret Cove Market. Yes Sah! She was meeting Baba-Lulla.

She got off the bus, her bosoms braced out ahead of her as she walked through the market where mangoes, pineapples and plantains were piled as high as Mount Diablo in the tangy afternoon light.

She edged her way through the crowds, looking for Estrianna, Lundie and Esmie. They were usually roun' about here, selling kerosene cans of black sugar and bankra baskets of fruits.

She saw groups of young girls in flimsy clothes and heavy jewellery. Stalls selling mobile phone covers and other bangarang things that she couldn't make sense of. People cotching-labrishing-sidestep-ping-hustling.

'Is not night-time,' she thought, 'But this yah light it strange.' She always knew what kind of a day it would be by the light. The way it penetrated the jumbled mess of her mind. Thin white light meant forgetfulness, a bright, blank page. This dark amber light was bitter-

sweet, thick with the flavours of old-time people, dead
and gone.

'Pound for four o' the carrots,' a man shouted, from
a face that was as long and yellow as a husk of corn.

She watched his mouth moving; it was too slow.

'Somethin' not right at-all-at-all-at-all,' she muttered.

She moved towards a stall piled with breadfruits.
The woman had a face like red-wash sandstone, dry
and peeling. Ready to split.

The breadfruits were lined up in the same way that
she used to line up the children every morning before
school.

She rose at five every morning, two hours before anyone else, and lit the paraffin heater in the back room.
Later, the children peeled off their pyjamas in front of
the heater, then took their places in front of their plastic basins. Each child had a different pastel-coloured
basin, which she filled with steaming water, and a
splash of bay rum. She lathered flannels with soap,
squelching the rags against the back of her wrist before
slapping it against their skins. She lined them up again
and took each face in her hands.

The thought of the children made her feel afraid.
They were far away from her. Why?

'You made your mind up, or what?' The stallholder
asked. The woman was heaving a sack of potatoes onto
the table with weather-beaten hands, crescents of dirt-
tipped fingernails. Muma-Miller looked at the coarse
dungarees, the t-shirt with the slogan 'Bullshit' splat-
tered across her chest.

'Oh, yes, ahhm, give me half o' the breadfruit please, maam.'

The woman pointed to a breadfruit. 'This do?'

'Them ripe?' Muma-Miller asked.

'Everything on this stall's ready to eat,' the woman said as she snatched the breadfruit up from the line and put it on the scale.

Muma-Miller leaned across and poked the bread-fruit, as she always did at Secret Cove.

'What did I just tell you!' shouted the woman. 'Didn't I say they were ready to eat. If you people go poking them, how'm I s'posed to sell 'em!'

Muma-Miller paused. Her eyes were brittle, the ginger heat of fear in them. She tried not to blink. 'Metal words stuck inna me head like machete,' she thought. 'Cyan't pull them out. What in God's name me forget now? Wheh me deh? Somebody tell me.'

She stood aside.

Not touch the fruit. Oh, yes, of course she was not supposed to touch them – that was the way things were done here. She held onto a stall selling mobile phones, swaying.

When the wicked advance against me
to devour me,
it is my enemies and my foes
who will stumble and fall.
...
even then I will be confident.

Her favourite prayer had popped out of the dark space in her head.

She looked at the young girls with their tight bodies

squeezed into skirts no bigger than the brown paper
bags the stallholders filled with their fruit. She smelt
the rich soil clinging to the roots of the vegetables.

She was not at Secret Cove Market, where everyone
touched the star-apples, warty soursop and sapodilla.
Rolled them in their palms, brushed them with their
fingers. She was not in Roaring River.

'Oh, Lord, the problems with the memory since
Poppa-Miller passed,' she thought.

She was an old black woman. An immigrant still.
Always ready with a pot of pigs' trotters or hominy,
singing stories at the empty Formica table.

'Poppa-Miller gone,' she thought. The Old Goat had
lumbered around the house for forty years aggravating
her with his bush habits. Him must have put obeah on
her – why else would she have put up with it! 'I going
tell the children that me no want to be buried with
him. I don't want to lay down with him for all eternity.'

Words and thoughts were bangarang – was she
thinking or speaking out aloud? Cho!

She left the market and caught the bus home.

She sat in her kitchen at the Formica table. She didn't
light the stove.

She thought of the country roads leading to Roaring
River; the shacks hanging off the lips of mountains like
a rebuke. The lilac and gold country light falling from
the heavens into the valleys.

Her body felt tired, the way it used to feel after a day
of breaking stones.

She picked up a pan and started beating the heads of
garlic with the base. Bruck! Bruck! Bruck!

Words left her head altogether and all she could do
was cluck-cluck-cluck at the base of her throat to keep

the fear away. She did that until she could see Baba-Lulla.

His body was very still. He had the same long face, the hooked Indian nose, the small chip in the chin that reminded her of a money-box. His eyes river-dark and wide.

'Come let me touch you,' he called.

'Oh man, you don't change,' she said.

He got up and came towards her. 'Boy, I only wish I could see you.'

'Man, yuh should be grateful you can't see me in this old age.'

'Look here, woman, just kiss me on me jawbone.'

She stood where she was. He came to her and took hold of her with his bony arms.

There was nothing strange about being held in his arms. She felt her youth being rocked out of the hard places in her body. 'Whoy, man, tek time! What people will say.'

'Millie, I can't see a thing, but I know nobody here to see us up here by the river. I only want to know you as you are here, now, sitting with me.'

'Man you always been too deep for me. Always up inna the air. Nevah practical.'

'And you was always worrying. And look yah – here you is.'

He held her and she could smell his hair tonic, citrus and bay leaf that smelt like the rainforest.

The shadows of the vegetation reflected on the river, like people swimming in the dark.

The distant rows of sugar cane thickened in the dusk, took on the shape of strange women levering forward with their hips, baskets of soapwood berries balanced on their heads.

'What people going to think if they find us here like this? Two old-time people playing the fool?' she asked him.

'No one gonna see,' he said. 'Check how me handle this yah wood.'

He gathered snakewood and split the wood length-wise with his machete. He lit the wood and layered it tightly.

Not a trace of smoke or flame could be seen in the dark amber light.

SKINNING UP

Southall, 1980

Riley stepped outside the shebeen. Steam was coming off her body. She pulled the grey rabbit skin jacket around her. It was cold and dark.

Five o'clock in the morning and she'd had enough of the dub and skanking.

'Where yuh goin'?' someone from a group of men called out. 'The party ain't done.'

The men were squinched together like quabs. Their silk shirts opened way down on their chests, like the cold was nuthn'; like it wasn't biting their raas.

'My bed's waiting for me,' Riley shouted back at them.

'Baby-love, my bed's waiting for you,' one of them called out. The men laughed.

'Yeah, yeah,' Riley said. She waved away their laughter. She could hear them siss-i-sissing behind her as she walked away, but she didn't business. If she didn't step, she wouldn't get back before Tutus woke up and realised her younger sister had taken her fur.

More importantly, Riley had to get home before

Muma, who was working nights at the old people's home at the back of the estate. Muma didn't know she was bustin' out of the house at night, going to blues parties and dutty shebeens.

But it was only a matter of time before she found out. Muma was cunning like that.

Riley crossed the road to the mini-cab office. She didn't have any money – never did. No matter, it was just one long walk up the Havelock Road – twenty minutes max.

She walked past the minicab office – the last sign of life – and turned onto the long dark road that wound past the cemetery on one side, run-down houses and wasteland on the other. In fifteen minutes she would reach the patch of grass that tried to pass for a park. She walked for five minutes.

The street lamps drip-fed bile-coloured light into the darkness.

She felt like a stix-gyal in the fur jacket, badn'raas. Invincible.

Not like that fool-fool Barry. He'd collected her that evening, driven her to the shebeen, promised to take her home.

Inside the club he pulled her to dance, winding and grinding against her, rubbing his sweaty face against her cheek. She shook him off. Left him winding up with some ugly bug-eyed gyal. Cho! She didn't business 'bout his dry-arse self and his mash-up car. She just wanted to get home and climb into bed with Crimpey, her little brother. His curled-up body was always warm.

She heard steps behind her. She stopped and turned.

It was Glendon.

Six-foot-four, slit-eyed Glendon who didn't skin-up with women or men. Every now and then he pulled a gyal off the streets and into his car. If the gyal was lucky he released her within a day or two. With or without her baggy. Every now and then he jooked-up a youth with his blade.

Riley's joints stiffened, but her brain was working hard.

'Yeah, w'happen, Glendon?' she said. 'Yuh come to walk me home, eh?'

Glendon kept slow-skip-skanking towards her.

'Looking out for me, Glendon, thanks.' Her voice was turning speakey-spokey. Don't lose it, she told herself. Play it real or you're in trouble.

'What's up, Baby?' Glendon said. 'Where you goin'?' He stopped a little way behind her.

'Back to my yard,' Riley replied.

'Forget that. Come back to my yard, mek we have a little drink and ting. You know dem ways.'

'Nah, man – I've got to step before my muma gets up.'

'Don't carry on them ways, Babe.' The slitty eyes flickered in his long dark face.

'Know what, Glendon, I appreciate you walking me home like this. It's kinda scary walking past the cemetery this time o' night. Nevah know what's going on back there.' She stopped walking.

Glendon looked over the cemetery wall. He looked back at her, and Riley could see he was unsure. Yes! She'd dropped the image right inna his head.

'Big-big man like you ain't scared of duppies,' she said. 'You've come to take care of me, make sure I get home safe, ain't you. I check for that.'

He stroked his chin, like he was thinking about something deep.

Riley wasn't sure how long she could carry on the skank.

Everybody knew that Glendon couldn't read or write. His parents left him in Jamaica when they first came over. The people he'd been left with worked him like a mule and he never went to school.

She carried on walking and he followed.

'Yuh look kinda cold,' he said. 'You know what I got at my yard?

'No.'

'Come on, guess. Something every girl wants.'

'Come on, Glendon, it could be anything. Just tell me.' She was trying to keep her tone light, friendly. 'Come nuh, man, what you doing walking behind me like that? How you gonna guard me if you ain't by my side?'

She didn't like the way he was walking behind, like he was tracking her.

'A fur coat,' he said, 'that's what I got. Black mink. Know how much that thing cost? Couple grand. Girl like you shouldn't be wearing no rabbit. You're betta dan dat.'

'Sounds crisp,' Riley said.

'Crisp? It's more than crisp. It's in the cupboard waiting for you.'

Riley didn't want to think 'bout no black fur coat hanging in Glendon's cupboard. She walked faster.

'Hold up, nuh, Baby. Why you stepping so quick?'

He caught up with her, pulled her wrist so that she was facing him.

'I could come over next week,' Riley said. 'I'm

bleached, I don't wanna come to your yard like this. I ain't fresh.'

'I don't check for freshness. I like things a likkle renk.' He put his arm across her shoulder. She could smell his sex; it clung to the back of her throat. She wanted to spit. But she swallowed it down.

'You're fit, you know dat,' Glendon said.

'You're fit too, like a sprinter or something,' she said.

'Not that kinda fit; you know what I'm talking 'bout,' Glendon said.

She had to try something else 'You believe in duppies?' she asked.

He splayed his fingers around the back of her neck like a brace. 'I don't believe in dem fuckeries!'

Riley knew he believed in duppies. People who said they didn't believe were just trying to protect themselves.

'My aunt Ermeldine is an obeah woman,' she said. 'Big time Obeah Woman. She brought all her sorcery with her when she came to this country. Everyone else brought their bangarang. She knew what she needed in this town.'

'Are you for real?' Glendon asked.

Riley took hold of the arm that was around her shoulders and moved it away, and linked her arm through his. Wasn't that how rich people linked and walked? People who lived good, knew how to behave. She couldn't out-run Glendon, she had to wrong-foot him. Skank him.

She felt his arm stiffen. Her arms and legs were trembling. She looked at him from the corner of her eye. He had the same bush features as her grandfather, Poppa-Miller: thick lips, wide nose, mallet-arms.

Glendon was like all the migrants from this slum town
– living underground, carving out their lives from
darkness. But Poppa-Miller was using his strength to
work his way up, to get to the surface. Glendon was
lost, working his way deeper and deeper down.

Sweet him, she had to sweet him up. 'Nice scarf,
Glendon. Burberry?'

'You know dat.'

'You always look crisp – you must be doin' alright.'

'I'm not gonna bust my raas like my muma, cleaning
shit for shillings,' he said. 'Cho, you gotta tek it.' He
swiped the air, grabbed a fistful of darkness and flung
it into her face.

Riley flinched; steadied herself. 'Your Muma live
round here?' Her voice was drying up now.

'The only place you should be thinking about is my
yard and that fur coat that's waiting for you,' he said.
His tone was harder now. They were getting close to
the turn off for Hunt Road, close to her house.

He wasn't gonna let her go much further.

She blinked – why had Muma come to this country?
Why hadn't she stayed in Roaring River, married some
old bush man who did nothing but dig up yams from
the rusty earth? A fur coat, to raas. Glendon was after
her skin.

They came to the large wrought-iron gate, the main
entrance to the cemetery. The other entrance was
on the northern side, close to the old people's home
where Muma worked. Riley thought of Muma in the
old people's home, pulling sheets up to the chins of old
white people with cracked, powdery faces. She thought
of her Aunt Ermeldine summoning duppies – fleshless,
boneless spirits.

'What the raas is that?' Glendon shouted.

Through the gates, Riley saw a small figure moving through the cemetery, not walking on the path, but cutting in between the gravestones, the shorter route to the gate. Head-down, moving quickly.

'What you done? What you done?' Glendon shouted, and he stepped away from her.

The figure came through the gate.

'Pickney, where yuh goin' this time a de night?' it shouted.

Glendon flexed his arms a little way from his sides.

'You t'ink I don't know you been crawlin' out at night like some dutty man?' the figure bawled.

Riley realised that Muma had been taking the short cut home through the cemetery, even though she'd told them all never to go that way – day or night.

'I'm gonna bus' your raaas when I get yuh backside home, yuh hear?' her Muma shouted.

Riley didn't answer. She could see that Muma wasn't really vex.

Muma was standing between her and Glendon.

Her Muma grabbed a fistful of the rabbit fur collar and dragged Riley to her side. Muma never once looked at Glendon.

Riley and her Muma turned their backs on Glendon and began walking slowly-slowly towards Hunt Road.

Styling it out.

BU'N UP

Southall, 2009

She hadn't seen him for almost thirty years, but it was him alright. She'd recognise him anywhere. The hiss an' sniff in dem green eyes of his.

'Ransford,' she called out.

The man stopped and turned in front of the row of ramshackle shops – butcher's, barbershop, pound shop. He was wearing picky-picky tracksuit bottoms tied at the waist with a fraying electric lead.

He stared at her.

She stepped towards him. She was an inch or two shorter now.

'Who's you?' he drawled, a funky roll-up burning on the edge of his lips.

'Ruby,' she said. He'd walked out on her a lifetime ago. 'Look like you could do with a drink. Come, nuh.' She pointed to the Gafun Café, two shops along.

'I know you?' His green eyes had a milky glaze.

They faced each other on the street. Migrants slopped past them in sandalled feet, jasmine incense drifting from side doors. Beer, urine and rotting scents coming up from puddles on the damp pavement.

'Eh-eh. Know me? Depends what you mean by "know".'

He shuffled behind her and they went into the café and sat at a table. A group of Somalian men were drinking coffee at a wooden table, shrouded in their body-bag clothes, shouting at the news blaring from a plasma TV on the wall above them. She saw blood-soiled bodies on streets pockmarked with black holes, and white dust. Crows circling the air.

'Me dream 'bout Johncrow,' Muma-Miller had told Ruby, just before Ransford left all those years ago. 'flying over yuh; tearing down the sky, the wings dem spread out blacka-dan-black.'

She hadn't listened to Muma-Miller's final warning, 'Me no like that man. If yuh fly with Johncrow, yuh will nyam dead meat.'

The café owner carried an earthenware dish of red curried lamb and flat bread to the Somalian men. He set down mugs of grainy black coffee for Ruby and Ransford.

'Where's your wife?' Ruby asked. She knew that Ransford had bought a house with his foreman wages; married a white woman called Sonia; lived with her in that stoosh town. The suburbs – she thinks that's what they call places like that. Green graveyards were what she imagined them to be.

With his light skin and straight hair, he could go to them kind of boasty places. Move up in the world.

He slumped in his chair, 'Don't know no Ransford. Don't have no woman.' He slurped the coffee and gargled, poked out his tongue. 'I scrape my tongue every morning. Scrape the white off it. Good for the health.'

She tasted a tang of the old fear in her mouth.

Machine gun fire on the TV. A white reporter with a helmet and bulletproof vest crouched down behind a wall talking to the camera, trying to style it out. Ruby recognised the fear of being hit.

'What you doin' back in these parts?' she asked.

'Babylon, we all in Babylon.' He pressed the cigarette stub back on his bottom lip and grunted.

Ruby looked at him and wondered at the power some women had to bring a man down. She'd only managed his tyres.

Ransford had visited Crimpey, their son, for the first six months after leaving. Brought him the usual wuthless things: trainers, tiny tracksuits. Nothing practical like food, or money for the gas meter. He hadn't showed up on Crimpey's first birthday. Or his second.

On the night of Crimpey's third birthday – thirty years ago – she'd gone to Ransford's fancy yard. She left the children asleep in the cold house, the old fridge humming in the darkness. It was January and the streets were slippery with frost. Fire for fire, she thought over and over, as she ran through the cemetery, across the rickety bridge to the railway station where she caught the last train.

She crouched down by the bronze Cortina that was parked in the pretty-pretty front garden. Remembering their nights – the smell of Old Spice and the damp, cloying scent coming from the pits of his body.

She jooked up the tyres of Ransford's car with her crochet needle. Stabbed again and again.

She watched the tyres crumple like black flesh onto

the earth. She walked to the high street and waited for the night bus. Snowflakes fluttered from the sky, fell on her face. She wiped them away.

The Somalis were talking, their turmeric-coloured teeth flashing. The café owner stood over them, shaking his head at the dead bodies in the street, and the vultures circling above.

'Your wife, your Sonia, she left you; that's what I heard,' Ruby said.

'Don't know no Sonia,' Ransford said. He looked upwards, 'God bu'n me if me lying.'

Ruby twisted her lips and clucked her tongue against her throat. That had been his favourite line back then. He'd throw his arms heavenwards and beg God to burn him if he was lying about the women's telephone numbers she found scrunched up in his shoes.

'Eh-eh, it look like God did well and truly bu'n yuh,' Ruby said.

'What a way your mouth fast,' Ransford said.

'Crimpey, your bwoy,' Ruby said quietly, 'remember him? Big man now. A musician. All my children doin' good. Professional people, yuh know.'

Ransford squeezed his eyes.

'Yuh cyaan milk your eyes for no memories, them inna yuh head,' she said.

'Shut yuh mouth,' he said.

Ruby looked at the long scrawny neck, the rings of scraggy flesh. She smiled at him. 'What happen to your house? Did Sonia tek it from yuh? Wipe you out good and proper, eh? Or did God bu'n it down?'

'Pretty lady, yuh tongue too red. It not healthy.'

A crowd on the TV had gathered around the bodies. They were wailing, tearing at their hair, their clothes.

The anger was still inside her. The doctors called it high blood pressure. Sometimes, she dreamt that she was using her crochet needles to jook the green of his eyes from the nerves in her body, drain the sour fluid that had pooled in her heart.

'You didn't think me and my children were good enough for you. And look now! Look how yuh come down.'

'No woman tek my yard. No woman.' He picked up the metal tray and beat his hand against it, again and again.

Ruby flinched.

'Pretty woman, pretty woman, don't be afraid.' He leaned across the table, his right hand coming towards her face, as if to stroke it.

The Somalis were looking at them. The café owner came over and took the tray from Ransford. He put his hand on Ransford's shoulder. 'Be still, my friend.'

Ruby's spine was tingling, the numbed aches coming to life. 'Yuh not sorry for leaving your son?' she asked.

'Me no have no son.'

'Everybody seh that you come home from your big-time job to see your Sonia winding her arse on some rich old man inna yuh bed. Mashed you up, didn't it. Bruck yuh mind.'

'Ruby?' he says. 'Pretty-pretty Ruby. Women always want diamonds and fancy things. Want-want-want. Tek-tek-tek.' He pulled the electric cord around his waist and knotted it.

'You chose some grabby-grabby woman. Woman who nevah dutty dem hands to live!'

'Woman must stay out of man business, ain't that so?' Ransford shouted to the Somalian men.

The men looked at each other, then looked away.

'Did you beat Sonia the way you used to beat me when she got up inna your business?' Ruby asked. She felt the old pain in her temple where he'd boxed her with his ringed hand until she'd seen fireflies flitting in the air.

The Somalian men were talking in their tongue.

'Yuh know damn well what I'm talking 'bout, don't yuh! Acting like yuh mad – that not fooling me,' Ruby shouted.

He stood up. 'Get outta here, gwaan 'bout your business, woman.'

'Your fancy uptown wife was with another man!' Ruby shouted.

Ransford stood up. 'You have no business here,' he said pointing to his head. 'This is my place. My place.'

'Your place? Your place indeed! It mash up, same way yuh mash up our house.' She thought of the windows loose from the times he'd busted them open when she had locked him out. The back door kicked in. She locked him out whenever he slept out, but he always kicked his way back in.

Until that last time. She had waited for him. The routine of fighting, sulking, locking-out, brucking in, was all she knew. She was sure he would return to his home, his flesh and blood – their flesh and blood.

Enid Blythe told her that Ransford had been seen in The Alhambra Restaurant with Sonia, wining and dining her. Takeaways from the Lahore Kebab House on her birthday was the best she'd got – if she was lucky.

Enid Blythe's husband told her that Ransford had been boasting in the Railway Tavern about how clean Sonia was, how she bathed twice a day, not in a plastic bowl with warm water and a rag, but in a bath full of hot water and scented bubbles.

'Yuh mash up me life! Say you're sorry for what you done,' Ruby whispered. She gripped the mug of coffee, wanting to dash it into his face.

'Pretty lady, drink your coffee.'

She looked at the yellow-green skin of his face – the colour of a three-day-old bruise. She remembered their final encounter. He'd flown into a rage because she'd served him corned beef instead of brisket. He'd taken hold of her hair, pulled her head back and tipped the plate of food over her face. 'What kind o' nastiness yuh giving me to eat? What the...'

The children stared, wide-eyed, terrified. That had been worse than the beatings.

She remembered the smell of the corned beef slithering down her face.

She could smell Ransford's renk odour. Past and present were right here, under her nose.

'Muma was right,' Ruby said. 'Me did eat dead meat, and look now.' She realised his absence had been large in the house, in her life.

She jumped up and went around the table and stood in front of him, looking down on him. She looked into his eyes, his green pupils in overdrive, widening. She saw a small dot of light in his pupils before it shrank. He blinked and looked away.

'Yuh gonna leave this earth and your own child not gonna bawl. Nobody gonna bawl.'

The café owner turned the volume down on the TV. Stood beneath the silent images with his fraid-fraid smile, holding the remote to his chest.

'Please go,' he said.

The men watched her.

Ransford shouted, 'I don't have no child; God bu'n me if I'm lying.' He jumped up, turned out the pockets of his tracksuit and pieces of crumpled paper fell out. 'Want-want-want. Tek-tek-tek. Tek it, tek what yuh want. Have it all,' he said, pointing at the pieces of paper on the floor.

Ruby looked up at the screen and the people's voiceless wailing. She looked at the men in the café. 'The man is leaving,' Ruby said and she pushed Ransford towards the door.

He walked out of the café, trailing the electric cable behind him.

HARD EARS

Southall, 2010

Crimpey stood with his two bredren on the railway track. They were leaning into the darkness like gravestones. They could do things like that with their bodies. He knew they could do more.

It was a cold New Year's night and they had come to platform zero where the freight trains ran. He was glad they'd left the dried-up house party, when only the two-stepping old-timers were left – tinsel dangling like nooses above their heads. Didn't they have children to go home to? Raases to bus', curses to cuss?

He stared down the track running through the town. Picky-picky snow on the padlocked sheds. Dim lights in the meat factory on the south side of the station. He felt the vibrations of the scheduled train that was many miles away; saw the windowless don't-fuck metal carriages, red codes emblazoned in red. Smelt the burning air.

'One more jump, then the shooting,' Mervin said.

'Come, nuh,' Crimpey said. He looked at Mervin whose jeans were hinged on gut-rope strength groin muscles. And Dregs, his other bredren, all sinnicky stout, swinging his hips, squeezing himself into the darkness.

'Where's dat train, Blood?' Mervin said.

'Soon come, I can feel it,' Crimpey said.

'Nevah mind what yuh feel,' Mervin said. 'Yuh see the sinting?'

'You're quick to think 'bout feelings when you're up in Mickisha's batty, though,' Crimpey said.

Dreggs leaned forward, crouching, arms on quads, spitting:

Mickisha, Mickeeeeesha,
release ya batty fast
Believe me, believe meee
Dis ya feeling
Nah go last.

They doubled-up laughing, torsos springing up and down like wind-up toys. Mervin, juddering shoulders crumpled into his ribcage, grabbed their hands and pulled them into a circle. His laughter triggered Dreggs whose head slid one way, body another; then Crimpey whose knees popped together liked magnets.

Bouncing up and down.

Up and down.

Crimpey heard their breaths in the darkness, felt the old cables above them twitching.

He could smell grease, metal, cooked meat from the factory. He shivered from the cool-burn of electricity inside his body. Like those green-black, weed-filled nights in his bedroom, playing his keyboard, singing for his life. Busking for the spirits that came to check him.

Listen, nuh,
Dem a my tunes
Wash belly pickney
Tangled up
Blue
My voice
That pulled you
Through…

His ears electrified like they are at the other circle he goes to.

He hasn't told his bredren about that circle.

There are no jumps at the other circle, only leaps of faith. Principles framed in gold. Crimpey has been going in secret for seven months. He whispers the principles to himself every morning, lying in his bed, staring at the psychedelic patterned carpet.

Spiritual Fatherhood. Personal Responsibility. Communion with Spirits. Retribution.

Every Wednesday night he gels back his coolie curls, slicks himself up in a black polo neck and black wool trousers. Pats himself down, checks his pimple-popped, pock-marked face in the mirror, widens his bullet-hole eyes, slaps himself in the face several times before heading out. He takes a bus and train to a town eighty miles outside the city – a town of glass houses that radiate white-light and other-worldliness onto the streets.

The spiritualist church is the only building on the street that is made of bricks. Set back from the road, Crimpey thinks it looks like one of those cottages in fairy tales where pickney never come out the same after they go in. If they come out at all.

Surgeon, Pilates teacher, policewoman, accountant, grief counsellor – these are the people in the circle. A dark wood-panelled room, burning candle, oil paintings of golden spirits with elongated bodies and limbs; black and white photos of old-time people sitting on chairs in frozen poses.

This circle does not hold hands. They don't body-pop. They're connected by belief in the principles.

Crimpey sits next to the Pilates teacher like he always does. An Australian with freckles all over his face, and snake tattoos writhing around his arms. They close their eyes and in the quiet he hears the rasping breath of his muma – her high-pitched-scatting-low-dread-tone. 'Bwoy, yuh too hard ears! Those who don't hear mus' feel.'

He hates the way she's afraid of everything; warns him away from everyone; refuses to answer questions about his poopa. She's afraid of life and she's made him afraid too.

He doesn't wanna hear her voice. He hears her first thing in the morning and last thing at night, complaining about the noise from the neighbours; the smell of poisoned dead rats lying on their backs in the alleyway. He wants to connect to his dead poopa, so he can ask him where the fuck he's been. Ask him about fatherhood and how to be a man.

He uncurls his fists, feels the air vibrating around him.

'I have a man with me,' the Australian says. 'A father figure. He's tall, lean. He's singing. Really going for it. Anybody take this?'

Crimpey doesn't claim the spirit. His poopa's name was Ransford, but people called him Bu'n-up. A black man burned out by life. Muma once told him – when, unusually, she was in an un-bitter mood – about his poopa's other nickname that people called him back-a-yard, in Calabash Bay, where he'd been a fisherman, carving canoes out of silkcotton trees, the way the Tainos built them hundreds of years ago. His poopa, she said, had been called ManFish because he used to dive deep-deep into the sea and swim for miles.

'What business man have inna the sea?' she asked.

From cool water swimming to bu'n out, Crimpey thinks. What a somet'ing.

'The spirit is waiting,' the Australian says. 'Anybody?'

No one answers.

The small candle burns out and the black wick flickers and twists inside the dying flame.

Mervin took three pulls, sucked the smoke through clenched teeth, then passed the skunk to Crimpey.

'New Year; new tunes,' Mervin said.

Crimpey looked at Mervin's resin-dark face and the hazel eyeballs too far out of their sockets. 'Everything's laid down for the tune. Just need that riff to mek it right,' Crimpey said.

'We're here, ain't we?' Mervin said. 'Fear is what our music's 'bout. Come mek we go deh, inna fear.'

'My muma's got that scene covered,' Dregs said. 'We can mek a move to her yard if we want fear."

'We should bring our moomas here; they know 'bout fear, but they ain't telling shit,' Crimpey said.

'True, true,' said Dreggs as he took the skunk from Crimpey.

Crimpey drew on the spliff, felt the cold air crackle and he swallowed something coarse and salty. Felt it enter his blood. 'Fix yourselves up. The train's coming,' he said.

The overhead cables twitched and sparked.

They gathered closer on the track. Mervin pushed Crimpey in front, stepped in the middle, Dregs behind. Their usual formation.

Crimpey saw the oncoming train in the distance.

'Hold tight, hold tight,' Mervin shouted, laughing. Crimpey felt the grinding of wheels on tracks, the undulation of steel on steel. The noise going down to the roots of his ears, dragging white light into his body. When the train was almost in his face, he saw his poopa, pixelated, then high definition – knife sharp goatee, Taino tattoos, head thrown back, jaw hanging open on some bitch-high note. Too high to hear.

There was an animal-squealing noise as the train hurtled towards them. Grinding, sparking.

They skank-stepped onto the other track closest to the platform on the other side, styling it out to the last second. The train missed them by a ghost's breath.

Crimpey stepped back onto the track where the train had just passed. Mervin was already swinging his legs back onto the platform. Crimpey looked back and saw Dregs stepping across onto the other track that ran parallel with the platform on the opposite side. He saw white light coming from the opposite direction. He jumped the track toward his friend, pushed Dregs out of the way. Screeching spirits brushed their faces.

Crimpey dragged Dregs across the track. Mervin helped him haul Dregs onto the platform.

Crimpey pulled himself up. 'Yuh got chigoe in your foot, or something!' he shouted at Dregs. 'Yuh betta move yuh batty betta dan dat next time or it's gonna be finger-fucking-lickin' fried.'

Dregs kept his head bent. He brushed down his trousers, patted his arms and chest. Then he wrapped his arms around his body. He was shivering, crying. Crimpey looked at Mervin; gave him the 'what de raas' look.

Mervin fist-bumped Crimpey. 'Wha'ppen, Blood; a you dat, playing hero? How the fuck yuh see dat next train? Come, rude bwoys, this yah is the fear we need for our music.'

Mervin slapped Dregs on the back. 'Dregs, stop being a pussy. Fix up fe the shooting.'

No one moved.

Mervin sucked his teeth and climbed back onto the tracks. 'Yuh batty-hole,' he shouted. He took a few stones out of his pockets, lined them up on the track.

Crimpey could smell something in the air, dank, rotting. A last breath. He swallowed it, felt it explode inside him. He jumped down onto the track. Lined up his stones and took Mervin's hand.

Crimpey kept his eyes open. He was feeling his music; feeling his poopa. Wanting him, wanting to show him. The black head of the train exploded out of the darkness. Death rattling along the track. Electricity sparked. The train licked the stones; bullet stones firing in all directions.

Crimpey was drowning in sound. It was like the sound of his own soul coming back to him. He exhaled, felt his body become light and bright; felt himself rising up and looking down at his bredren. Dregs lying motionless on the platform, something like black river sand gushing from his head.

Heard his poopa's voice saying, 'Swim, bwoy. Swim.'

THE CRYPT

Southall, 2013

She knew it probably wasn't his thing. Firefly lights flashing in the limestone crypt. Crimpey and his crew spewing duppy sound dub from their witchcraft machines.

'Psychoacoustics, straight to my frontal lobe,' Rocco said to Tutus.

'You won't survive,' she said. 'Unless you drink the white rum.'

He put the glass to his lips and she watched him drink.

Six months since she'd last seen him, and she couldn't stop thinking about his naked body last night – withered muscles, flaccid flesh. And he'd cut off his long black hair. Nothing but grave-dust hair on his skull.

She had to take him here. Their shadows had to darken the metal stairway that took them down into the Crypt. Cocktail mixologists, trustafarians with insouciant up-do's and bush-man beards – all talking bad. Everyone was talking bad these days – only it wasn't bad any more.

They had an alcove to themselves, a little cut off from the crowd. She wanted it that way. They drank, talked; he kissed her, but his tongue was listless in her mouth – a stranger with nothing to say.

Crimpey's voice on the mic. 'Yeah, yeah, big shout out to my sister, Tutus. She's here with her Latino man, all the way from Jamdown. Respect to the elders.'

The crowd at the bar cheered.

Witchcraft music kicked in again: echoplexed screams and rimshot thunder.

'Maybe the past is frozen over for a reason. Digging it up from a river in Siberia might be bad luck,' she said.

'You sound like the old women in Roaring River. Twenty thousand years ago? When did those ice migrants travel to America? This is the opportunity that won't come again,' he said in his singing-shushing voice.

'Cho! You're more interested in the dead than the living.'

'Look at this place. Listen to your brother's music – full of ghosts. You are superstitious, afraid of ice.'

Tutus imagined Rocco in the white nothingness of Siberia, dangling from a guide line in his black wetsuit – a tadpole embedded in striated ice.

Yes, she was afraid of ice – afraid of rivers. It hadn't always been that way. She remembered the last time she'd seen him, back in the spring. He'd stopped off in Roaring River for ten days, en route to an archaeological conference in New York.

Out on the river, a cool, misty morning in April, Rocco

leading her away from the rushes and stones, out into the water.

'You must know the river if you want to take your guests swimming and canoeing,' he said. Tutus had set up a small bed and breakfast at the house, which Baba-Lulla had left to her.

Rocco took her hand and they waded out until the water came up to their necks. Tutus looked back at the riverbank of mangrove trees and up towards the mountains, dark and solid as zemi gods. The last thing she heard was the rattling call of jacana birds.

Underwater, close to the surface, the river was the colour of bay rum and silvery-cool.

She let go of Rocco's hand – or had he let go of her?

She swam a little way down towards blue tinctures bleeding out of limestone. Saw the dark underbelly of the river, vegetation coiling and twisting.

An undercurrent churned up sludge and sediment, pulled her into the dead-pace flow.

She kicked and twisted, struggled for breath, and in the disturbed murky water she saw Mikey's body, white and puffed up as cotton, floating between the river weeds. Only it wasn't Mikey's face, it was Lorne's childhood face gleaming with the coconut oil that Muma-Miller used to rub into it, polished, like the trophy she'd wanted him to be.

Tutus kicked harder, pulled towards the gauzy light at the surface, but she swallowed the water, breathed water into her nostrils. Spinning and sinking, as Muma-Miller, Baba-Lulla, and Marisa bubbled into life, foamed and dissolved into the sludgy darkness.

She thrashed; heard the slur of breath in her head; saw the warping of water, light and time.

Peace.

The music stopped. Crimpey was talking on the mic again. Rocco was talking to her, she could hear his voice, but she could still see Lorne's face. Lorne was ill and she had come back to Southall because he wasn't expected to last until Christmas.

'Something is happening to me,' Rocco was saying. 'Going to Siberia changes everything. I have to clear my head and heart before I go. When I come back I won't be the same.'

She looked at him. 'Your bald head will freeze in Siberia,' she said. 'You look like a penitent.'

He started to sing.

Una va pasada
Y en does muele
Más molera
Si mi Dios querrá

One glass is gone
And now the second floweth
More shall run down
If my God willeth.

'The sailors of Cristobal Colon sang this on their voyage of discovery,' he said, 'when things became difficult.' He drank more rum. His eyes were red and watery. 'How is your little business in Roaring River?'

'Three burnt-out professionals are there. Orsorio and his wife are taking care of things. It's all good,' she said. 'Guests swinging in hamacas on the verandah. They've escaped the recession, the riots. And here I am, back in Southall. And there you go – again. Why did you come here? Was it just to end everything?' She looked at his empty glass.

'You're following your trail; I'm following mine,' he said. 'That's the way it's worked for us.'

They listened to the music. A peeny-wally, wiry man came into the alcove. He cotched on the stone bench, stroking his chin, his lips pushed out and twisted in a vex-up pout.

'Yes, Blood, want something for the night?' The man asked.

Rocco smiled and shook his head. The man moved closer, flexed, cut his eyes on Rocco.

Rocco's eyes narrowed, his cheekbones rose up like blunt tools. Tutus put her hand on his arm.

The man kissed his teeth and left.

'He was as dangerous as ice,' Rocco said. He laughed.

She wasn't laughing, but she wouldn't let him hold her the way he'd held her after that day at Roaring River.

'You shouldn't stay in Southall too long,' he said. 'You don't have a home here anymore. Things change very quickly.'

'I love Lorne,' Tutus said.

'Love like that is a good thing,' Rocco said.

'And other love?'

'Love is love.'

'I grew up looking up to Lorne with my child's eyes. That way of looking at someone goes deep. Love should go deep.'

Rocco said nothing.

'I'm going to see Lorne tomorrow. I'll move between Muma's place and the old house. I don't know when I'll come back to your hotel.'

'I understand.'

The damp chalky cold seeping out of the limestone made her shiver. It would be hard seeing Lorne in the old house. She imagined Muma-Miller's house – dark and empty, inhabited by prayers rather than people.

'That house tugs at my guts, like a current,' she said. 'I suppose there isn't a place that does that to you.'

'Forget haunted houses.'

He said he would get more drinks and she watched him walk out towards the bar.

Crimpey was playing a dub-step tune. A girl in a bronze-coloured mini was talking to Rocco. She was winding-up while she talked, her breasts and batty calibrated to the drum and bass. Her hard young face caramelised in foundation. Rocco looked back at Tutus and shrugged, 'What can I do?'

Tutus picked up her bag and walked towards the bar. She pushed between the girl and Rocco, went eye-to-eye with him. He moved towards her but she blocked him with one hand.

'Go dig up the ice. Gwaan 'bout yuh business!' She heard Muma-Miller's voice echoing back at her, a ghostly dub-plate effect.

She swung her bag over her shoulder and walked up the wrought-iron stairway, past the bull-necked bouncers. She marched through the courtyard, crossed the road onto the bridge that led to the old town. She walked along the tow path to Bush Tea Canal. The factories in the distance were silent. Shut down long ago. She remembered the day that Mikey had drowned, the day that Lorne had sent her away.

She remembered the sunlight, the hurt.

She was afraid of losing Lorne. It would be like losing Marisa. She couldn't lose Rocco – a man like that belonged to the past – but she was afraid of the pain that would come. She saw everyone in Rocco's indigenous beauty – the Lullas, the Millers, the Sleifers, the Siberian ancestors.

She needed Roaring River, the valley filled with light, the land braided neat as Muma-Miller's scalp.

She looked across the canal. There were only a few barges. Most people had sailed west up towards the River Colne. Disappeared like Mikey's father. The canal was the colour of black cane juice.

Tomorrow she would go to the old house to see Lorne.

The light in the back yard will fall on Poppa-Miller's wild herb bushes. The back room where Muma-Miller used to have her prayer meetings will still be haunted by old spirituals, like Sunday evenings in Roaring River when the voice of the congregation carries along the river.

She will go there tomorrow. She will dash white rum in the corners of the rooms, the way Poppa-Miller used to do.

She will not cast the spirits out.

She will ask them to stay.

To always stay.

COOL BURN

Roaring River 1908

Mrs Lulla is sitting on the steps of the barracks. It is harvesting time, and the north wind has set in. There is blackness in her heart. Blackness blooming across the cane fields. Long-time-back smoke rising.

The overseer's bell rings out across the plantation. Five more hours loading trash onto the carts. Five more days burning cane. Three more weeks before her husband will be freed. She squinches her eyes against the black smoke and looks at the labourers sharpening their machetes. They are standing under the extended roof of the labourers' barracks. From the moment their feet touched the island they were not the same.

Nor was she.

'Accha! Let them sharpen.' Nothing was sharp and dark as the kohl around her eyes, which flicked up at the corners like horns.

She *aiiiee-aiiieee's* to the dancing girls squatting by the chulah, rolling chapattis. They twirl wrists, jangle their beaded necks in response.

She slurps ganja tea from a bowl. Smacks her lips, clenches her eyes as the ganja lights her gut.

She is taken back to the cold of another lifetime. And there he is, the same husband.

'Why does he follow me through lifetimes?' she asks aloud. 'With that long face of his, hollowed-out like a begging bowl!'

She cannot remember her name in that lifetime of creaking ice islands, but she thinks she was the same as she is now – tiny, wire-waist; bead-eyed. Holding out a piece of charred wood, she tells her same-husband, 'Put protection around your eyes.'

They are standing at the edge of the ice-jumbled Chukchi Sea. Blue sun. Indigo sky. In the distance, black fur-covered specks walk on the smoking ice, loading canoas with blubber and chaga.

'Wife, listen to me,' the same-husband says. He pushes the charred wood from his face.

'Fire protection for mind,' she says.

He grabs the stick, throws it onto the ice. 'We will be cursed if we leave.'

'Spirit can go anywhere,' she says. She looks beyond at the ice floes floating south, glinting with the promise of unknown worlds. Behind them lie the wet-sedge meadows and shallow ponds of their Siberian village. Some of their people refused to leave. They lit peat fires and prayed for the souls of those departed. Watched as the Katabatic wind covered their tracks.

She cannot feel what happened next in that lifetime. They must have boarded the canoas because the next thing she sees are storms in the sky. The hollow of her same-husband's face becomes the night-sky filled with star dust.

He did not make it to the new world.

Mrs Lulla drains the ganja tea, takes a handful of roasted cashews from her lehenga and shakes them in her hands like dice. 'If I bury same-husband again we will meet in next lifetime. Again, again,' she thinks. She knows she must save her same-husband if she is to be free of him in lifetimes to come.

She knows, too, that the tin roof prison that he is in will boil out the little life that is left in his bones.

She throws the dregs of the ganja on the ground and twists her small bare feet into the damp earth. The labourers walk past, their machetes glinting. Staring at her, black juice seeping from their burning eyes.

Later in the night, when all the men are sleeping, it is safe for her to climb into her cot, but not safe to sleep. She keeps her small lantern burning. Nothing more than a rotting partition board separates her from the labourers in the barracks. She hears their chests rattling; smells their breaths and overheated bodies.

Her same-husband is in prison for running away.

He'd chopped his way downriver, trying to get back to the sea, to India. To Hariharpur.

His chiggoe feet and hookworm belly hadn't taken him far.

She dreams far and wide with her eyes open. Dreams her dead, wart-riddled mother is throwing scalding cane juice into her face, screaming about the shame of prison.

Mrs Lulla gets out of her cot, her face burning.

'Who are you to say this?' she hisses to her dead mother. 'You had no shame.'

She remembers how, as a small child, she ran away, trying to get beyond the vermillion dust of Hariharpur.

Her mother would drag her back by her hair, shouting: 'Worthless girl. You bring shame!'

Her mother – henna-haired, nose-ringed and bull-headed – was the most shameless woman she had known. There was no one her mother would not bribe. Nothing and no one she would not sell.

Nothing too small to avenge.

Mrs Lulla leaves the barracks, goes out into the foggy night air of the mountains. One or two fires are still burning in the cane fields. White egrets fly close, swooping and pecking at the insects that fly out of the flames.

With quick, small steps, past the boiling house, the mill and trash houses, she drags the angry face of her mother behind her.

She comes to the Big House. She believes that Massah Sleifer is one kind of man in the cool comforts of the plantation house and another in the accounting barracks where he spends his evenings during the burning time, close to the smoke and stench. And why not? Hadn't she been another person in her mother's mud hut in the village of Hariharpur?

Who was she now?

She can no longer see her dead mother's face, but she can smell her cardamom-and-amla-oil spirit in the smoldering air. 'Go!' she hisses.

She goes up the wooden steps of the accounting barracks and steps inside. An old-time plantation whip hangs on the door, its cowhide tail swinging.

Massah Sleifer looks up from the dim light of the desk lamp. He sees her and his mouth turns up like a sugar bowl. The accounting books are open in front of him. Half a bottle of white rum, a plate of gizadas.

She stays close to the door.

'Too many men in the barracks, Mrs Lulla?'

'I cannot sleep without my husband, and with the sour breath of men in my face.'

He stands up. 'Plantations need women, not wives.'

She holds out her hands, palms upwards. 'You have taken my husband. I am in the hands of God.'

Massah Sleifer gets up, walks away from the pool of lamplight by the desk and his squat shadow rises up and follows. He points to fireflies hovering inside the room by the open jalousies. 'Look there, they take refuge from the cane fires. In my father's time, life here was different for our women. We held great dances in the Big House. Our women wore fireflies – alive. Living jewels of fire and light. All women are fire, I think.'

Mrs Lulla takes the whip off the door. Runs a section through her fingers as if she is assessing the finest silk. She imagines the burn of it against skin. 'You are the one turning day to night with black snow,' she says.

'Mrs Lulla, you are not a preacher and I am not the converted. I know what you want. You people think I am hard, but the authorities don't want crimes to go unpunished. Your husband stays in his prison.'

She wonders whether with one-two-three *lassshhh*, like a Goddess, she can transform the room. But there is no fire in her, only smoke.

Massah Sleifer gives her a glass of the rum and she drinks it.

'Ganja better for my spirit,' she says.

'Rum keeps the ghosts away,' he replies. He puts his glass on the side table.

She knows he will not speak of the thing that all the labourers are talking about: the strike on the Seaford estate, on the other side of the island. The plantation manager had been killed trying to stop a riot. His skull had been broken. His eyes taken out.

She squinches her kohl protected eyes on Massah Sleifer. If she takes out his grey eyes with the tail of the whip he would stop staring at her. He would stop saying, 'You people!'

She walks towards the jalousies, looks at the living jewels weaving trails of light in the smoky air. Like the lighted ghats on the river near Hariharpur.

She left Hariharpur with her same-husband two years ago. They travelled by bullock cart to Calcutta in the summer, through saffron dust storms and thunder. Spent three weeks inside the walled New Garden Depot where she hawked and spat from her dry throat, afraid to drink the globby water that was drawn from tanks.

'Everything has the hand of God in it,' she said to her husband as they went into the agent's room. The recruiters in the yard below were shouting, 'No dwarfs. No scarecrows!'

She felt sure her same-husband would be told he was a scarecrow. Her mother had called him worse, even though she had promised her to him, an old-man Dholi, when she was eight.

The agent sized her same-husband up with an east-to-west shake of his head. 'Wiry-tough is good. Go to your fortune.'

Mrs Lulla pressed her thumbprint on the indenture warrant. Her husband was as still as a votive figure.

She lashed her hawker's tongue at him, 'Bhains ki aulad boot-nee ka.'

'Chup! Chup!' He shouted. He did not look at her as he pressed his thumbprint on the warrant that neither of them could read.

A week later they boarded the SS Ganges, a steamship loaded with scribes and weavers, soldiers and dancing girls.

Four months later they arrived on the island. A truck ride through forested mountains, before the final ridge from where they looked down at a flat valley. A twisting, silver river. Massah Sleifer's sugar plantation.

Massah Sleifer pulls her back, tugs her onto the day bed beside him. He takes the whip from her hand and places it on the pillow as if he is putting it to sleep.

She hears the cries of crickets and cicadas escaping their burrows in the bush of the lowlands.

Massah Sleifer takes her face between his hands and squeezes until her black-protected eyes bulge.

She sees that his eyes are filled with the numbers of his accounting books. She holds his stare and the numbers fall from his eyes and she is able to see the darkness of his own journey, the migration of his German people a hundred years ago from their land. The same tin tickets, rations. Crowded steamships with rotten partitions that did nothing to protect their women.

Massah Sleifer pushes her onto her back.

She thinks, 'This grinding season. All cutlass thrash and thrust. Breaking my body for land. What have I become?' She remembers her mother's hawker tongue.

'Grinding season hard,' she says. 'Plenty cane to cut, Massah Sleifer.'

He is on top of her. 'Two hundred and eighty acres,' he whispers in her ear, 'seventeen point one a piece. I will give you two days holiday when all is done.'

'Strong hands not easy to find in these times,' she says. 'And we Indians good at strike.'

'What is that you are saying?'

'We can strike good, like the Indians on Seaford plantation.'

Massah Sleifer rolls over, sits up, clicks his wrists. 'Woman, don't play with me tonight.'

'It is bad when an honest Indian is put in prison like a criminal. It is a great shame for our people. The Indians say they will strike.' The Indians had not said this, but she decided she could play with numbers too. 'If Indians strike, you have to hire Creoles for harvesting, and them is more shillings than a Coolie.'

Massah Sleifer takes the whip and lashes it at the fireflies, breaking up their trail of light. 'Madam Lulla, take your husband tomorrow. But be careful. Plantations can be dangerous places for wives.'

'God is good.'

She does not go back past the Big House, or the cane fields. She walks towards Roaring River village and crosses the old Spanish bridge to the river.

Women stooping at the shore, lighting votive boats, placing them on the river where they sail south into darkness.

She is not sure what lifetime she is seeing.

ABOUT THE AUTHOR

Jacqueline Crooks is a Jamaican-born author. She writes about Caribbean migration and subcultures and has received an Arts Council England Individual Artist award for her writing. Her individual stories have been shortlisted in the Asham Award and Wasafiri New Writing competitions and have appeared in: *Virago* and *Granta*; the Woven Tale Press; and *MsLexia*. Crooks has an MA in Creative and Life Writing from Goldsmiths University. She delivers writing workshops to socially excluded communities, primarily older people, refugees and asylum seekers, disadvantaged children and young people.

ALSO AVAILABLE

Jan Lowe Shinebourne
Chinese Women
ISBN: 978-1-84523-151-4
Prince £8.99; pp. 100; pub. 2010

Told through the eyes of Albert Aziz, a Guyanese Indian Muslim, the story opens with his boyhood memory of falling from a tree and being badly injured, after which he develops a compelling attraction to a young Chinese girl, Alice Wong, who lives on the same sugar estate. Now, years later, Aziz is a highly paid engineer in the Canadian nuclear industry. Although he has a new and prosperous life, he still nurtures racial resentments about the way he was treated as a child and has become a supporter of radical Islam. He also begins to fixate again on Alice and tracks her down. He finds that she is divorced and living in England and asks her to marry him. Though Aziz is telling the story, it is clear that Alice's apprehension is slowly mounting as she fears the consequences of what might happen if she turns him down.

David Dabydeen
The Intended
ISBN: 978-1-84523-013-5
Price £8.99; pp. 246; pub. 2005

The narrator of *The Intended* is twelve when he leaves his village in rural Guyana to come to England. There he is abandoned into social care, but with determination seizes every opportunity to follow his aunt's farewell advice: '…but you must tek education…pass plenty exam'. With a scholarship to Oxford, and an upper-class white fiancée, he has unquestionably arrived, but at the cost of ignoring the other part of his aunt's farewell: 'you is we, remember you is we.' First published almost fifteen years ago, *The Intended*'s portrayal of the instability of identity and relations between whites, African-Caribbeans and Asians in South London is as contemporary and pertinent as ever. As an Indian from Guyana, the narrator is seen as a 'Paki' by the English, and as some mongrel hybrid by 'real' Asians from India and Pakistan; as sharing a common British 'Blackness' whilst acutely conscious of the real cultural divisions between Africans and Indians back in Guyana.

"Painfully beautiful and true" – Maya Angelou

"Essential reading" – Caryl Phillips